The Whispering Man

The Whispering Man

Henry Kitchell Webster

MINT EDITIONS

The Whispering Man was first published in 1908.

This edition published by Mint Editions 2021.

ISBN 9781513283555 | E-ISBN 9781513288574

Published by Mint Editions®

minteditionbooks.com

Publishing Director: Jennifer Newens
Design & Production: Rachel Lopez Metzger
Project Manager: Micaela Clark
Typesetting: Westchester Publishing Services

Contents

I

Not in the Papers

It is strange that we should have been talking about Dr. Marshall that very night, I and my new friend and neighbor, across our little table in the restaurant. Talking about him we were, and at considerable length, too, before I bought the paper that had the news of his death in it. But, after all, it had come about naturally enough.

Jeffrey and I had made friends, I think, for the simple reason that we were about as unlike as any two moderately intelligent and successful young men could be. Well, there is no use stretching my own modesty to cover Jeffrey's position, too. He at least was more than moderately successful in his vocation, which was that of a painter. As to intelligence, it was a discussion of that very subject which had led to the introduction of Dr. Marshall's name.

Arthur Jeffrey was an illustrious monument to the deceitfulness of appearances. He looked like a rising young stock broker. Except among people whom he could really call his friends, he made no impression, and aimed to make none, except that of a brisk, alert, well-mannered, perfectly dressed young man, whose habitat for seven hours of the day was, no doubt, somewhere below Chambers Street. I think it would have been hard to induce the desk clerk at the fashionable apartment building off Madison Square, where we both lived, to believe that Jeffrey, when he emerged from the elevator so promptly at half past eight every morning, went uptown, instead of down, to a big barnlike studio, where he painted pictures whose queerness and daring were making him the talk of New York.

But, if he was all commonplace on the outside, he was pure genius within. I have never known a man who so deliberately and consciously abandoned the faculties of logic and reason, which he nevertheless possessed in a high degree, in favor of the more hazardous flight of fancy.

I suppose it was because he discovered no streak at all of genius in me that he took a fancy to me. What reputation I may have attained for myself as a lawyer and as the author of a large calf-bound text-book on evidence, has come to me through the exercise of the very faculty, to which my friend was fond of alluding in terms of such contempt, the faculty of thinking straight and consecutively.

It seems he had heard, possibly from myself, though I am inclined to doubt it, of this textbook of mine on evidence, and some unaccountable freak had induced him to buy and read it.

During the hour we had sat there over our dinner, he had amused himself and me by attacking, with a wealth of audacious paradox, one after another of the principles of evidence which my book contained. They were not, for the most part, principles which I had formulated myself; many of them were as old as the common law, but the most venerable of them all was none the safer, on that account, from my friend's attack.

"What does the best evidence in the world amount to, anyway, when it comes to that?" he concluded. "It's utterly meaningless, except when it's tied on behind some theory, like the tail on a kite. As for expert testimony, there's only one kind of true expert, and he is just an inspired guesser, no more, no less."

"Come," said I, "take, for instance, Dr. Roscoe Marshall, who is, perhaps, the leading alienist in the United States. He has probably taken the stand as an expert in more insanity cases than any other man. Well, go and buy his book and read it—his book on mental and nervous diseases. You'll find it more interesting than mine. And see how much guesswork you think there is about that—Why, what's the matter with you? What are you chuckling about?" For my friend sat there, enjoying a silent laugh all to himself, as if what I had just said had been something exquisitely amusing.

"Drew," he said at last, "never argue with a man who always has the luck on his side. You are delivered straight into my hands by your own illustration."

"I don't see how," said I.

"No, but you will. Listen. I painted a portrait of Mrs. Marshall this spring. She's a great beauty, by the way. She must be at least twenty-five years younger than her husband. Did you ever see her?"

"Yes," said I. "I know her rather well. She's his second wife."

"Well, that has nothing to do with the point. Marshall liked the picture a lot, so much that he offered to pay me more than the price I had agreed to paint it for. Of course I wouldn't take that, but I asked him a favor instead. I wanted some casts made of his hands. He has the finest hands I ever saw. He finally assented, and I've got them up at the studio now. I'll show them to you some time. Well, that has nothing to do with the point, either. The advantage of not pretending to be logical is, that you can wander around as much as you like.

"Anyway, that's how it happens that I was talking to this famous expert of yours only this morning.

"I had happened to tell him once that I believed that I always knew a criminal when I saw one, without knowing how or why—by just looking at him. He didn't scout that theory as you would if I were to give you the chance. He said he could recognize an insane man in the same way. He said that only the other day a man came into his office to consult him about some little nervous affection he had. The man's manner was quiet, composed, to the normal eye perfectly normal, but he knew, just by looking at him, that the man was mad—mad as a March hare. In a year, or less, he was willing to stake his professional reputation, that man would turn into an out-and-out lunatic. The queer part of it was, he said, this patient was a doctor himself, and he, obviously, never dreamed of his condition."

"That's a rather grisly idea," I commented. "But what's that you say about yourself: that you can spot a criminal in the same way, just by looking at him?"

"Oh, I shan't attempt to make you believe it," said Jeffrey easily; "yet, if it weren't against my principles, I could offer some evidence to prove it."

"Waive the principles without prejudice," said I, "and give me an instance."

"Did you know that I was once a newspaper artist?" he asked me. "Of course I came out strong at murder trials and such places, where the staff photographers couldn't get in. In that famous Marshbank's trial—do you remember it?—I attended every session of court, and I knew who the real criminal was from the first moment. If I had been the judge, instead of bothering to select a jury composed of the twelve stupidest men in the city, I should simply have pointed out the respectable gentleman, who was the star witness for the State, and said, 'Take him out and electrocute him,' and that would have been the end of it. It wouldn't have taken ten minutes. It came to the same thing in the end, but it took two years to do it, and wrecked an innocent man's life in the bargain."

"And you believed all the while," I repeated incredulously, "that McWilliams was the man?"

"Not believed; knew. Oh, I don't know how. That's the whole point. That's what I've been preaching all the evening. The only certain knowledge is the inspired guess."

There wasn't much room for argument with a man who took that position, and I was glad when the arrival of a small newsboy crying the eight o'clock extras in the street outside afforded an opportunity to change the subject. It was a warm evening, toward the latter part of May, and the doors were open, so I called him in.

"We'll get down to something important," I explained as I did so. "We'll see how the baseball game's come out."

But the black headlines that caught my eye had nothing to do with our great national game. I was conscious, while I stared at them, of a queer sensation, that might almost be called a presentiment.

"That's rather curious, considering," said I, handing the paper over to him.

For the item of news I had read there, which tried to make up by the size and blackness of its type for the meagerness of detail which it afforded, was that Dr. Roscoe Marshall, the famous alienist and specialist in nervous diseases, had been found dead in his office chair at half past twelve o'clock that afternoon.

We made some pretense at reading the rest of the news, and talking about indifferent subjects, but neither my mind nor his succeeded in getting very far away from the main theme.

Finally, after a little silence, I remarked: "There is this to be said of him, he was absolutely on the square. Nobody in the world had money enough to get him to cut an opinion to fit the brief. There are precious few experts who won't do that. The State Attorney's office will miss him."

"Well," said Jeffrey, "I am glad I've got those casts of his hands. They are both distinguished, the right and the left one. I never saw such a pair."

It occurred then to both of us, I think, that we were treating the memory of an illustrious citizen rather inadequately.

"Of course," said Jeffrey, "I knew him very little. You knew him rather well, didn't you?"

"On the contrary, not well at all. I know her—knew her, I should say, as I've hardly seen her since she married him. I knew her—rather well."

"In other words," said Jeffrey, "you were once in love with her. Well, that's natural enough."

It was natural enough. I think that all the men who ever enjoyed the privilege of knowing Madeline Cartwright well were more or less in love with her, and I had been no exception to the rule. The rule which I was an exception to was that the men who fell in love with her generally got over it when they found that their feelings toward her were not reciprocated.

I was in the habit of assuring myself, with a good deal more confidence than I actually felt, that I had got over it, too; but I had never gone so far as to be able to imagine for one moment that I was in love with anybody else. At all events, I had made small progress toward carrying out her injunctions of a half a dozen years ago, that I go away and forget about her. She had said it in perfectly good faith, but she had said other things on that memorable night that would have made forgetting impossible to any but a man of brass.

"We don't miss it by so very much, Cliff," she had said. "I have hoped to come to feel toward you the way you feel toward me. I'd like to if I could, and I have—well, kept you along in the hope that I might; but it's no use. We don't miss by so very much, but we do miss somehow. Some day a man may ask me whom there is no question about. I don't know whether there is such a man in the world or not, but if there isn't, I shall never marry, Cliff."

Well, I wish to Heaven she had kept to that resolution. After that I had pretended to her, and to myself as well, that my feeling toward her had cooled down into the comfortable sort of affectionate regard which she felt for me. I think my pretense deceived her, though it never was very successful in deceiving myself.

It was about two years ago now that she had confided to me that she thought of marrying Dr. Marshall, and had asked me what I thought of him. Of course I had not committed myself on a dangerous subject like that, but she had no difficulty in seeing, I imagine, that I regarded it as a mistake. So it was altogether natural that, when she went ahead and did it anyway, our relation should have lapsed. Of course I said nothing of all this to Jeffrey, but I did not deny the validity of the guess he had hazarded.

"I would like to know what you thought of him," said I, "or, rather, what you thought of them together."

He was ready enough to talk, at all events. "Take it altogether, I think she's in luck. They were a queerly matched couple. Oh, disparity of years had nothing to do with it. They fascinated each other about equally, but while he was really in love with her—as well as he knew how to be, and no man could be with her every day and not be that—I think that in the core of her heart she hated him."

"Hated!" I cried in protest. "Come, draw it mild."

"Not a bit of it," he resumed. "Marshall was a queer mixture."

"He was a cold sort of fish," I admitted.

"But not like the other cold fishes. Most people are cold just because they can't understand. Understanding, sympathetic people are nearly always warm-hearted. If you can really stand in another man's shoes and see how the world looks to him, it generally makes you like him. But it didn't have that effect on the doctor. He saw through everybody; knew why they laughed at this and cried at that; knew how the world must look to them, but that knowledge never warmed him up a bit. Human souls were just so many specimens to him, possessed of more or less scientific interest. His wife's was the most interesting one of his collection, but that's all it came to. Why, of course she hated him."

Somewhere along in this conversation we had left the restaurant and started strolling across the square toward The Atlas, where our apartments were. Its brilliantly lighted entrance was now in plain view. In the full light of one of the great ornamental outside lamps we could see two persons in apparently earnest conversation. One was the hall boy. You could tell him even at this distance by the glitter of his cut-steel buttons. The other figure looked familiar, too, though I probably should not have recognized it had it not been for the present theme of our conversation.

I quickened my pace a little. "Do you know," said I to my companion, "I believe that's his son there now."

"Marshall's? What's he doing here?"

"I can't imagine, unless he's come to see me. He's been attending a course of evening lectures I give at the law school, and I've come to know him pretty well in the course of the last few months. He'll take this hard, I suspect; harder than anybody else. Come, they'll have told him I'm not there, and I'm afraid he won't wait. Do you mind hurrying a little?" But the figure had disappeared in the dark before we had come near enough to attract his attention.

"Too bad you wasn't a minute sooner, sir," said the hall boy, as we came up. "There was a gentleman here, very anxious to see you. Ah—there he comes back now."

I wheeled around, to confront a white-faced young man, with wildly haggard eyes.

"Mr. Drew!" he cried; "I've found you at last!"

I grasped his hand and his shoulder at the same time, to steady him. "You needn't tell me," said I; "I've seen the papers. Do you want me? I'll do anything I can, of course."

"Yes," he said; "Mrs. Marshall does, and I do, too. She suggested sending for you. I've an electric cab here waiting. Can you come at once?"

"In two minutes," said I.

I turned to make my excuses to Jeffrey, but found him listening in his turn to the conversation of the hall boy:

"There's a gentleman waiting for you in the reception room, sir; he's been here some time; says you expected him."

"Send him up to my apartments," said Jeffrey; "I know who he is." And without turning in our direction, he walked straight to the elevator.

Young Marshall and I made no attempt to talk until we were rolling along uptown in the late physician's electric brougham. The relation between Marshall and me was hardly that of pupil and professor. That is a relation I like to avoid, and in this young man's case I had succeeded. We were almost like older and younger brother.

I laid my hand on his shoulder. "I know there is nothing I can say that will make it any easier—"

He gave a sort of dry sob at that, and my grip on his shoulder tightened. He was shuddering all over. The impression I got was one of horror rather than of grief, somehow.

"You don't know," he said, when he had commanded his voice. "It isn't in the papers; not the worst of it." And then he turned and looked me full in the face, and the wildness of his eyes startled me. "It isn't in the papers yet," he repeated, "but it will be—I think—oh, more than that—I know. My father was murdered!"

II

Madeline

All I could do at first was to repeat the word after him, in an accent of horror as profound as his own, "Murder!"

He sank back limply against the luxurious leather cushions, and turned his face away. "Yes," he whispered.

My mind, which had simply stopped running at the shock of the word, swiftly recovered itself and went to work again. "But how?" I asked. "What was the weapon, and who could have been the murderer? Who in the world had a motive for wanting to murder him?"

"There was no weapon," he said.

"No weapon? Then how was the murder committed?"

"I don't know." His voice was quite lifeless. Evidently it was with the greatest difficulty that he forced himself to talk at all. But I wanted to know more than he had told me, as I did not care to face Madeline until I did.

"If there was no weapon," said I, "and you don't know—"

"Oh," he interrupted, with a trace of impatience; "I don't know, really. Dr. Armstrong, when he first saw him sitting there over his desk, thought it was heart failure. But it wasn't that. Even I could see it wasn't that from the look in the eyes. There was the wildest, most horrible glare. And then they called down Adams, whose office is on the floor above, and he disposed of the heart-failure theory at a glance."

"What did he say it was?" I asked.

It seemed as if the young man beside me would never be able to frame the single word needed to answer my question. He struggled with it, but for a long time it would not come. When it did, it was only in a whisper. The word was "poison."

Now, the idea of sudden death by poisoning has a peculiar atrocity about it such as no other death-dealing device contains, for poison as a means of murder spells treachery in burning letters that even a child could read. It is a means of murder no avowed enemy can use. A man may be stabbed or shot in a heat of passion, or even in self-defense, and by an enemy who has taken a brave man's chance of meeting the same fate himself in place of his intended victim. But poison can only be administered by a false friend. So I did not wonder that the word was a long time coming from my young friend's lips.

Presently, however, I thought of something; hesitated a while whether to speak of it or not, but finally decided in the affirmative. "I suppose," said I, "that it's an idea that would be hard for you to entertain, but if he died by poison, isn't it altogether probable that he administered it himself? To speak plainly, don't you think that he committed suicide?"

"Hard for me?" he echoed, with a half-hysterical laugh. "Good God! if I only could believe it! But it's perfectly impossible. My father was one of the happiest as well as one of the sanest of men. His nervous balance was never disturbed, and had, indeed, very little to disturb it. His whole life was an open book, and there's nothing in it we don't know. He was rich; he was famous; he was altogether happy in his work. He was looking forward with special interest to some cases that were coming up within the next two or three days."

"Did you see him this morning?" I asked.

"At breakfast, yes, as usual," he answered.

"And was there anything unusual or abnormal about his manner?"

He hesitated an appreciable space of time before he answered. "Nothing abnormal—no!"

I noticed by the slight, unconscious emphasis that he put on the word that he avoided denying that there was anything unusual. But he was obviously in no condition to be catechised, so I let that point go.

"He went to his office at his usual time?" I asked.

"Yes," said he, "and found the reception room full of patients waiting for him, just as he always did. He saw them in rotation up to half past eleven. At half past twelve they found him—dead."

"Then," said I, "the patient who went into his office at half past eleven was the last person known to have seen him alive?" But before the question had fairly passed my lips, I realized that it was little better than wanton cruelty to ply him with questions and compel him to make answers in his present condition.

He made no attempt to answer this last question at all, but buried his face in his hands and let the shuddering sobs, that all along had been threatening his voice, have uncontrolled sway. He made a brave effort to regain his self-control, and presently succeeded far enough to be able to stammer out an apology to me for the exhibition he had been making of himself. Before our swiftly moving vehicle had reached his father's door, he seemed to be somewhere near himself again.

The house was an ordinary four-story brown-stone affair, furnished with exquisite taste, and in no way suggesting the profession of the man who had owned it. Dr. Marshall's offices were a good deal farther downtown, in the Grosvenor Building, and, to a far greater extent than most physicians find it practicable to do, he had made a practice of locking his work up inside his office every night.

There was a large living room, half library, half den, in the rear of the second story, and it was hither that young Marshall led me. Two or three young men, whom I took to be reporters, were waiting in the front drawing-room, and their curious glances were fixed on me as I passed the door on my way up the stairs.

The upper hallway was dark, so I could not see who it was who addressed my guide from the head of the stairs, but I did not need to see; I should have known that voice anywhere.

"Did you find him, Jack?" she asked. But she did not wait for his answer, for the next moment she caught sight of me.

"It was good of you to come, Clifford Drew," she said. That was an old characteristic of hers I well remembered, calling me by both names, and she offered me both hands when I had gained the last of the stairs and stood beside her. "I thought you would not fail us," she added. "Come in."

She led the way into the dimly lighted library, her stepson standing aside to let me go in first. She did not seat herself until she had crossed over to the wall switch and flooded the room with light. That action was characteristic, too, and, in a way, symbolic. She had never courted twilights or concealments. If she had anything to conceal now, the thing it would hide behind would be a mask of absolute candor.

I was glad to have a good look at her now, after those two years. She was all my memory had painted her; just as beautiful as ever—more, I think I may say, for her beauty had only come to its full, matured perfection. She was a large woman; magnificent, calm, stately. Her head was crowned with a glory of chestnut-brown hair, shot through with metallic lights, and her eyes matched it. They were brown, but quite without that velvety dullness which detracts from the beauty of so many pairs of brown eyes. Hers were extraordinarily bright and singularly expressive. The impression of intensity that one got from her came, I think, almost exclusively from her eyes.

Her manner certainly was repose itself. She was still dressed in the simple lavender-colored house frock she had on when they brought her the news of the tragedy. It would have been hard to imagine a manner more exactly opposite to that her stepson had exhibited, than hers was when I stood looking at her across the library. Her eyes showed no trace of tears, nor were they stony, fixed, paralyzed with grief or horror, as many tearless eyes are. Her hand, as she withdrew it from the wall switch, was as steady—I had started to say as mine; it was a good deal steadier.

But for just one instant I saw a look of apprehension come across her face. That was when she glanced toward the doorway, where her stepson was still standing.

"I suppose you know the story," she began. "Jack has told you, hasn't he?"

"I couldn't tell him much," said he, from his position in the doorway. He seemed not to mean to enter the room, but her attitude invited him. "I tried to tell him, but I gave it up."

"Well, don't worry any more, Jack," she said. "There's nothing you have to do now. Can't you read, or do something to get a little quiet, and then go to bed? Clifford will attend to everything."

"Exactly," said I; "that's what I'm here for. I'll see everybody who is to be seen, and answer questions as well as I can."

Of course I meant what I said, but I was a little surprised and rather unpleasantly affected by the eagerness with which the young man accepted my offer. He muttered a barely audible "Thank you," turned, and went straight up the stairs to the floor above, where his own room was. A moment later I heard his door close behind him with a bang.

"Of course," said I, "it must be a fearful blow to him." She made no answer, but then my comment called for none. "And, after all," I continued, "I think he has told me nearly everything. He said that Dr. Marshall went to his office this morning, as usual, and saw an unbroken succession of patients, until within an hour of the time they found him dead. There are only two or three other questions that I should have asked him had he been in condition to give me all the information I wanted. One is, who was the last person known to have seen him alive? The patient who went in, I believe, at half past eleven?"

"I don't know much about her," said Madeline. "She called up the house on the telephone only about an hour ago, having just learned that Dr. Marshall was dead. She said she would be glad to tell us anything she could about him. She is a Miss Gwendolen Carr. She gave me her address, and I've written it down. I don't suppose she will be able to tell us anything. She had a nice voice."

The thing I was wondering about all the while was, what her own explanation of the tragedy could be, and it seemed impossible, seeing her sitting there so tranquilly, that she could believe the terrible theory I had just heard advanced by the dead man's son—murder by poison. I hesitated even to suggest it to her in so many words.

"I understand," said I, "there is some disagreement between the two doctors who saw him as to what had been the cause of death; that one of them called it poison, and the other attributed it to heart failure."

"I don't think there can be much real doubt about it; in fact, Dr. Armstrong has practically admitted that he was mistaken."

"By the way," I asked, "who is Dr. Armstrong? How did he happen to be there?"

"Why, didn't you know he was Roscoe's assistant? He has had that position for nearly a year. He was right in the adjoining room all the while."

I looked at her in wonder, for she stated this momentous fact quite as if she saw no exceptional significance in it. Yet if murder had been done, as my young friend believed, and murder by poison, who could more easily have accomplished this fiendish act than the trusted young assistant with an office in the next room? Could he have any motive for such an act? I would make further inquiry about him presently.

For the moment, however, the alternate theory, suicide, presented itself very strongly to my mind. I asked Madeline the same thing I had asked of Jack in the cab, "Did you see anything unusual or abnormal about him this morning at breakfast?" But this time I got an answer; it was unequivocal.

"Nothing abnormal, but unusual, yes, decidedly."

"Jack hinted as much to me," said I, "but seemed not to want to talk about it. Do you mind if I ask you more particularly?"

"Jack hinted at it?" she repeated. "How could he have known anything about it? Why, no, I don't mind telling. He and I—Dr. Marshall, I mean, and I—had been having a somewhat sharp difference of opinion for a day or two past, and it came rather to a climax this morning."

"Was your quarrel serious enough," I asked, feeling my way with a good deal of hesitation—"serious enough to have afforded a possible motive for—" I hesitated over the word, but she manifested no such squeamishness:

"Suicide?"

"Yes."

"No," she answered quietly, "not by any possibility. I don't think it would have amounted to anything that could have been called a quarrel, if he hadn't been tortured with indigestion at the time. I didn't know that till I saw on my dressing table the capsules he always takes. Anyway, if it had been my own quarrel I shouldn't have pressed matters. As it was, I had to, for I was trying to dissuade him from doing a great wrong to someone else."

I could not help it. It was not a suspicion of her; it was a wholly involuntary perception that the story she was telling me was forming itself into a pattern.

I couldn't get my own voice to come very clearly when I asked her the question that was on my tongue. "Who was it," I asked, "against whom he meditated this wrong? If there has been murder, there must have been a motive for it."

She paled a little, but she answered the question steadily: "It was Dr. Armstrong."

Do you know what I thought of then? I wished my friend Jeffrey might have had the opportunity for the long, straight look she allowed me right into her brown eyes. Was it a face of the most courageous innocence, or of the most cynical guilt? Would Jeffrey know, I wondered. Evidently she saw that I did not, for as she read what was in my face, I saw come into hers the same expression of quick apprehension I had seen there when she was looking at her stepson. But she came a little closer to me, and held out her hands with a quick, appealing gesture.

"Cliff, do I have to pretend with you? Can't I let my looks and my inflections, and all the ghastly perverse inferences that could be drawn from the things I have been telling you take care of themselves? Does it matter to you that I haven't been crying, or do you think that I ought to have pretended not to be able to talk about it calmly, even if I was?"

"No," said I. "I am glad you are not pretending at any rate."

"I didn't poison my husband," she said quietly, "and I don't believe Dr. Armstrong did. You were right, dreadfully right, when you advised me not to marry him. I never was in love with him; I often hated him, or thought I did. But I shall miss him dreadfully. Can't you understand that? And yet I am not altogether sorry that he died today. He's had a good life, a full life. It has brought him everything he wanted—wealth and fame, and all the rest of it. In going out now, he's prevented from doing a man a serious wrong, a young man for whom life otherwise seemed to have as much in store as it had for him. I had tried to get him not to do it. I urged him to show a little plain, unmixed, undeserved mercy, but he wouldn't listen. That quality wasn't in him. He had done once before, years and years ago, before I knew him, the very thing I was trying to prevent. He had pushed a brilliant young man off the edge of things; a young man who only needed a steady touch of the shoulder to set him right. Instead of that, he was sent slipping down, down, down, quite off the curve of the world—our world, and in what miserable slough he perished, I don't know. I ventured to remind Dr. Marshall of that young man this morning. That was why he went away in anger."

After she finished speaking, she made a listless gesture with her hands, as if it didn't much matter after all, and went back to her seat. "But, as you perceive," she continued, a hard, lifeless tone of satire in her voice—"as you perceive, the pattern is quite complete. Walter Armstrong has been making love to me—I am just telling you how it looks—and the doctor and I have quarreled about him; and the doctor went down to his office and died of poison, with Dr. Armstrong in the next room, and with a little box in his pocket containing the capsules which he had forgotten and I had handed to him, in the presence of the butler, before he started out. That's reasonably complete, isn't it?"

Whatever had been in her voice and in her face before, there was nothing there now but hard defiance. "Do you advise me to lie," she concluded, "or dare I tell the truth?"

The sharp jangle of the telephone bell broke the long, tense silence which had ensued upon her last bitter question, for I had not been able to make an answer to it.

I went to the 'phone. "Is this Dr. Marshall's residence?" asked a voice. "Well, this is Police Headquarters. Can we talk with Mrs. Marshall?"

"No," said I. "I am representing the family. My name is Clifford Drew. I'll take your message."

"Well, we've got the man," said the voice at the other end of the 'phone. "I don't think there can be any doubt about it. He's Pat Pomeroy. He's one of the highest class crooks in the country. He was in the doctor's office this morning pretending to be a patient. We arrested him about an hour ago on suspicion, and found a large unset ruby in his pocket. We think it's the Marshall ruby, and we want some member of the family to come down and identify it."

I said that we would come, and hung up the receiver. Then I turned to Madeline. "Thank God!" I cried, and I gave her the message. I felt somehow that I could breathe again; that the heavy black pall which had hung over my spirit since young Jack Marshall had inarticulately uttered the word "poison" was suddenly torn away.

It was wonderful that the police explanation had occurred to none of us. Dr. Marshall had been a connoisseur of precious stones. He was known to have a hobby for them, based upon the reactions they produced on certain classes of patients. He frequently exhibited them to the mentally disordered persons who came to consult him, and the fact was more or less generally known.

But Madeline's face showed hardly the relief I expected to find there.

"It's all right," I went on, trying to reassure her. "The pattern that we fancied we saw forming itself about you is knocked to pieces. The only possible doubt of Pomeroy's guilt will be settled when we identify that ruby in his pocket as Dr. Marshall's."

"Well," she said, "perhaps you are right."

III

The Theory of the Police

I decided that Jack would be the best person to take with me to identify the ruby, and leaving Madeline in the library, went upstairs to his room. Also, I was anxious to relieve his mind of the horrible idea which I supposed he had shared with me, and which I took to account for his distracted conduct in the cab.

I knocked briskly on the door, and entered the room without waiting for his invitation to come in. He was still fully dressed. "Well, it's all right," said I. "They've got the murderer. I guess there's no doubt about it."

His face, which had been pale before, went white as chalk. "Who? Where?" he asked. "What makes them think so?"

"It's all right," I repeated. "Sit down and listen. There is nothing more to worry about. The man who did it is safe under lock and key in the police station."

I thought I heard him say "the man!" after me, in a whisper. When I turned quickly upon him to verify my guess, however, his flushed face and bright eyes seemed to be trying vainly to conceal the relief he was ashamed to show.

"It's queer," said I, sitting down on the edge of the bed, "that none of us ever thought of robbery as a motive. But while we were sitting here, torturing ourselves with all sorts of weird and ghastly suspicions, the police were quietly at work rounding up the professional criminal, who, beyond any doubt, will prove to be the guilty man. You can identify your father's great ruby, can't you?"

"Yes," he said, "of course I can." He got up at once, set his somewhat disordered clothing a little to rights before the mirror, and started for the door.

"Stop in the library on the way down," I suggested, "and speak to Madeline. It would please her, I think, and certainly she deserves it."

"What do you mean?" he asked, turning to face me at the door.

"Why," said I, not knowing just how to put it, "of course she saw what both of us were thinking of; she knew that we couldn't help being aware how the circumstances pointed at her."

"At her?" he repeated. "Who are you talking about? What do you mean?"

"I mean Madeline, of course," said I a little impatiently. "Both of us made fools of ourselves. I've acknowledged it. I was suggesting that you do the same thing."

He looked at me for a moment with a perfectly blank stare, made as if to speak, and checked himself. Then, without a word, he opened the door and walked ahead of me downstairs. He did go into the library and speak to Madeline.

"I am glad it's all right, stepmother," he said. It seemed that this half-humorous fashion of address was one he always used.

"You are a dear boy," she answered, laying one arm across his shoulder. "You couldn't help it any more than Cliff. By the way, there's another telephone message come for you. You are to go to the office in the Grosvenor instead of to Police Headquarters. They've taken the prisoner up there."

The Grosvenor is a modern office building running up to a moderate height of fifteen or eighteen stories, and is situated just off the Avenue in one of the cross-town Thirties. It is luxurious to the last degree in all its appointments; and its tenants were the residuum of so keenly discriminating a selective process that the roll of them was altogether imposing. That the respectability of the Grosvenor should be presented to the public eye in the yellow press, in the same black headlines with the words Murder and Mystery, struck me as one of those ironical little jokes that Fate is so fond of playing.

I thought of something else, too, as young Marshall and I were taking our places in one of the battery of quick-firing elevators with which the building was provided, and this was a theme I had heard Arthur Jeffrey dilating upon only the other day—the modern office building as the theater of Romance.

"No writer of modern fiction," Jeffrey had said, "need ever go to the deserted moor, or the forsaken farmhouse, or the abandoned mine working for solitude or for mystery. The modern office building can beat them all at that. One can come and go in them unseen, unremarked, by the other hundreds who are coming and going also, each bent on his own private, peculiar concerns. If you want to commit a crime, do it in an office building. You are as good as a thousand miles away from the scene of it once you have closed the corridor door on the room where it happened. If you want to meet a long-lost brother, here is the place to do it; he may have had an office on the floor above for the last five years. Its resources in the way of surprise, terror, mystery, and, yes, picturesqueness, too, are absolutely unrivaled."

Making due allowance for my friend's fondness for paradox and exaggeration, there was still something in what he had said, I thought. In this case, however, the murderer had evidently found himself at the end of a short tether. If he had acted on Jeffrey's advice, he had profited ill.

By the time I had reached that conclusion, we were out of the elevator and had opened the door into the reception room where Dr. Marshall's patients had sat waiting that morning, and where they would wait no more.

The doctor's suite of offices was L shaped, occupying, as it did, the most desirable and expensive corner of the most expensive floor of that most expensive building. Dr. Marshall's own quarters, subdivided into an office, an examination room, and a dressing room, occupied the corner itself, flanked to the south by the large reception room we had just entered, and to the west by the smaller office of his assistant. The reception room and the two offices each had an independent door opening into the corridor, and both the reception room and the office of the assistant communicated directly with the doctor's. So much I had been able to observe, or had already been told, on crossing the corridor and entering the reception room. I was to learn more about it presently.

The reception room was furnished with a magnificent Oriental rug, a large mahogany center table, littered with magazines and books, and a number of easy chairs. Also a telephone desk, where the attendant sat taking messages, making appointments, and sending into the inner office the patient next in line, when the sound of the doctor's buzzer announced that he had just dismissed the preceding patient into the corridor. There were two telephone sockets in the desk, one for connecting the wire into Dr. Marshall's office and the other for the assistant's.

A man in a police sergeant's uniform, a burly man with a big mustache, was sitting at the telephone desk when we entered the room. There were some other people sitting about in the various easy chairs, but I had no leisure to examine them particularly just then.

"My name is Drew," said I, addressing the sergeant, "and this is Mr. Marshall, who will be able to identify the ruby, in case it proves to be the one that belonged to the doctor."

"The lieutenant will be out in a minute," said the sergeant. "He's in there." He nodded as he spoke toward the door to the inner office. "I'll let him know you're here."

He suited the action to the word, but said, after a moment of cryptic conversation into the transmitter, that we were to wait. "There's plenty of comfortable chairs and there's no hurry," he added philosophically. He seemed rather bored himself, however, for he yawned portentously when he spoke.

"What's the lieutenant doing in there?" I asked.

"Sweating Pomeroy," he answered laconically, apparently surprised at so unnecessary a question. "Trying to get a squeal out of him." I took it that he used the word "squeal" in the highly technical sense of confession, rather than in its looser literary sense.

"Is all you've got against Pomeroy," I asked, "that you found a ruby on him? Supposing that it is the ruby, what made you think he had it?"

He hesitated about answering me, seeming to think that discretion required a discouraging amount of reserve on his part. But he really wanted to talk, and he really was proud of the way the police had caught up and run down their clew.

It seemed that O'Malley, of the traffic regulation squad, had seen Pomeroy at the corner and recognized him, and after walking half a block toward the Grosvenor entrance, had seen him turn in there. He had reported this occurrence to the roundsman, with the result that as soon as it became known that Dr. Marshall's death was a coroner's case, probably of murder, two and two were put together and Pomeroy was arrested in a resort he was known to frequent. He was searched, and what appeared to be Dr. Marshall's great ruby was found on his person. His description also tallied closely with that furnished by the reception-room attendant of an alleged patient who had come in and waited for some time for his turn to see the doctor, and then gone away, apparently without accomplishing his purpose.

"She's sitting over there now," said the sergeant, lowering his voice, "and we are going to give her a chance to identify him presently, as soon as the lieutenant gets through with him."

"Who are the others?" I asked.

"Oh, them? They're some more patients who were here in the office when he was supposed to be. We'll let them identify him, too, if they can."

“What I don’t understand is,” said I, “supposing Pomeroy did get in there with the purpose of stealing the ruby, why he should have poisoned the doctor, or how he could have got him to take it.”

“Poisoned nothing,” said the sergeant easily. “He suffocated him, that’s what he did, and he didn’t mean to do that, most likely. Just gagged him to keep him quiet, and pushed the gag too far back into his pipe.”

Before I could question him further on this totally new theory of the case, the sound of the buzzer recalled the sergeant’s attention to the telephone. After listening to the unintelligible half of a brief conversation, we were told we could go in now to the inner office.

I crossed the room at once and opened the door, under the impression that Jack was at my heels. When I looked back I saw him still standing beside the desk.

“Come in, if you want to, and shut the door,” said the lieutenant.

“My name is Drew,” said I. “I am not the man who can identify the ruby. He’s out there.”

“Come in anyway,” said the lieutenant, “and shut the door. We aren’t ready for him yet.”

I seated myself in the nearest chair and looked about me, but the first sensation I experienced came not through my eyes, but through my nostrils—the strong acrid smell of stale tobacco. What made me notice it was the knowledge of the late physician’s fastidious aversion to this very odor. The detective force had been making free with the place for hours. There were enough of them here. There were five or six men in the room, including the one who must be the prisoner, and the man at the desk, whom I took to be the lieutenant.

They were all in plain clothes, and with due deference to the personnel of the detective force, I am obliged to admit that it took me a minute or two to satisfy myself as to which of the other men sitting about the room was the prisoner, and which were the guardians of the law.

Evidently, this device was a deliberately produced effect, for the lieutenant now spoke through the ’phone to the sergeant at the desk outside. “Send in the girl,” he said, “the telephone girl.”

Evidently they meant to identify the prisoner before proceeding to the identification of the ruby.

The girl answered the summons. She was a young woman of no particular characteristics, unless, perhaps, her hair had the look of being somewhat more blond than nature had made it. She came in with a good deal of confidence, which visibly and rapidly ebbed, however, as her gaze traveled from one face to another of those about the room.

After looking more and more vaguely at the faces of the men who were paraded for her inspection, she turned, as if in despair, looked long and earnestly at me, and finally focused her gaze on the lieutenant himself. "I think," she said at last, "it must be one of those two." She had not included me, as I half expected she would, for evidently her powers of identification had failed her completely.

"'Think?'" said the lieutenant. "This isn't a case of thinking. Do you know?"

In spite of his efforts, he could not galvanize her into even a reasonably firm conviction. She was an indisputable failure, that was all there was about it. So she was dismissed into the corridor, and "the one with the black eyes"—this was the lieutenant's mode of designation—summoned from the outer office to replace her.

Her eyes weren't black at all, those of the girl whom the opening door now admitted. They were the greenish-gray, curiously brilliant, and never twice exactly the same, that are so often seen, half veiled behind long, down-drooping black lashes. Her hair was black, too, and so was the small toque she wore, and the severely tailored coat and skirt, which set off so beautifully the perfections of a small, slender, well-poised body. She was well shod, something which cannot be said of all women more expensively and elaborately dressed than she; and I got the impression, though she had not removed her gloves, that her hands must be beautiful. At any rate, there was a distinction about the way she carried them, and about the slight, almost imperceptible gestures she made with them which gloves could not disguise.

It was hardly five seconds before she spoke. "The second man from the right end was in the office this morning," she said. "He was wearing a small mustache then, and different clothes."

He was the one I had already guessed to be Pomeroy, though of course I had never seen him before. I had founded my guess on the fact I had noticed, that just before either of the two attempts at identification, while the other three men had not changed at all the attitude in which they had happened to be at the moment, this man had drawn himself a little straighter, as if he meant to give himself an authoritative, quasi-military air.

Evidently the identification was correct, for the lieutenant was trying to conceal his pleasure in it. "You are sure of that, are you?" he said. "It's not a guess?"

"Yes, I'm sure," she replied. "If you will look at the little finger of the right hand, the hand that is in his pocket now, you will see that it is bent out at the last joint as if it had been broken."

"That's all right," said the lieutenant, "and you're all right. I wish there was more like you."

For a moment my attention had wandered from the criminal and the effect of the identification upon him. I was thinking about the girl's voice. How thoroughly it pleased and satisfied the ear, even in the utterances of the few words I heard her say; and I was trying to recollect what I had heard about a nice voice earlier in the evening. Then it came to me. This was the girl who had telephoned to Madeline—Gwendolen something—the last person known to have seen Dr. Marshall alive. She, too, had been dismissed into the corridor before I had completely identified her.

"Send in the old guy," the lieutenant was saying into the telephone. "That was a good identification, but we may as well have another."

IV

Carlton Stancliffe

The man who had entered the room in response to this last summons proved agreeably disappointing to my expectations. My interest in the proceedings, which had somehow flagged after the disappearance of the girl in black, was revived again instantly by the sight of the newcomer. As he is destined to play a large and most romantic part in the solution of our mystery, and as his queer, brilliant, eccentric personality is to appear very often in these ensuing pages, I think I may be pardoned a description of him.

He was the sort of man who never would be spoken of as old, if it were not for his attempts to look young. He was actually, I should judge, somewhere in the middle forties, a tall, graceful, and commanding figure, with a strikingly handsome face. There was nothing weak about it. The features were big and boldly, though finely, modeled, and the deep-set eyes singularly expressive. The only fault one could find with him was that he carried everything just a little too far. He was too aggressively well dressed; too painfully clean shaven; his manner a little too dignified; his voice and features a little too expressive. It came upon me all at once what he must be—an actor. That was it. Everything about him was heightened just enough to carry itself over the footlights. He was in evening dress, wore an overcoat and gloves, and carried a walking stick, as well as an irreproachable silk hat, in his hand.

Like his predecessor, he identified Pomeroy instantly. "That's the man," said he, pointing at him with his stick. "He was the third patient to come in after me this morning. He was sitting in the reception room waiting his turn when I went into the doctor's office."

Up to the middle of that last sentence his voice had been just what I should have expected an actor's to be—rich, suavely inflected, perfectly under control. But just at the end of the word "reception," it suddenly abandoned him, and he completed the sentence in a queer, harsh, voiceless whisper. The suddenness of it startled all of us, but it did not seem to surprise the man himself.

He turned to me with a faintly apologetic smile. "It's a curious vocal affection," he said, still in that harsh whisper. "I am never able to be sure of finishing a sentence audibly. I am one of a good many who have reason to regret Dr. Marshall's death. He held out hopes that the difficulty was not incurable."

Curiously enough on the word "incurable," his voice came back again.

My attention was diverted then by the entrance into the room of my young friend Marshall. Why Jack had not come in sooner, I did not know. He had heard, evidently from the sergeant outside, of the successful identification of Pomeroy. The effect of this had been to brighten his eyes and bring a good clear color into his cheeks again.

The whispering man had seated himself beside me, evidently with the intention of seeing the little play out to the end.

Young Marshall walked over to where the lieutenant sat. "You have something for me to identify?" he asked.

"I understand," said the lieutenant, "that your father owned a rather well-known ruby. Do you know where he kept it?"

"Here in the office, most of the time," answered the young man.

"And you saw it often, did you?"

"Yes."

"So that you might expect to know it when you saw it?"

"Yes, without a doubt."

"Isn't this it?" The lieutenant's hand opened as he spoke, revealing in the palm of it an enormous, blazing red stone.

We had all automatically drawn nearer. The other detectives, the whispering man, and I were now gazing alternately at the great stone itself and the thoughtful young face that was bending over it.

"That's it," said Jack.

"You'd identify it on oath?"

"Yes," said Jack, "I'd do that."

"That's all, then," said the lieutenant. He turned to the sergeant, who had by now come into the inner office. "Call the wagon," he said, "and take him back." And then he uttered a word of valedictory to Pomeroy. "You see we've got it on you," he said. "You might better have owned up yourself."

I guessed from that, that his efforts to extract a confession from Pomeroy had not been successful. This surmise was correct, for from the moment of his arrest he had scarcely spoken a single word, had declined to offer any explanation whatever of his visit to the doctor's office, or of his possession of the ruby.

There seemed to be no further need of my going back to the Marshalls' house that night, so I sent Jack home alone, with instructions to tell Madeline that the murderer was certainly caught, and with the promise from myself to be on hand the first thing in the morning. He seemed glad enough at the prospect of a little solitude, at which I did not wonder.

It is strange to think of, but it is true, that our attitude toward each other at that moment was almost one of congratulation; yet we were standing in the very room where, not twelve hours before, a great and famous man had met a sudden and appalling death, and that man was the father of the one who had just so cheerfully extended his hand to me in parting.

I doubt if he had ever proved himself a very affectionate parent. You could hardly imagine the word Affection used in connection with him. Yet that was not the reason for the quick rebound our spirits had made. It was the unutterable horror of the explanation of the crime which had forced itself into both of our unwilling minds—his, I was sure, as well as mine. After contemplating that possibility for a while, the fact of the murder itself seemed of secondary importance. Having found the motive for it to be simple robbery, and the murderer himself to have been a hardened criminal, seemed almost to make all right again.

And yet after Jack had gone out I stayed there in that inner office. Saw them take the prisoner away; saw everyone go, including the lieutenant himself, leaving the premises in charge of the young policeman who was to keep watch during the night.

And standing there alone, the actual tragedy, savage and horrible enough, though it was not so unspeakably inhuman as the one my own imagination had constructed, began, for the first time, to assume a reality for me.

I saw the doctor sitting there, calm, unsuspecting, in the full tide of life and work, allowing himself, perhaps, a moment's leisure to enjoy the pleasant memory which that last patient of his, the girl with the darkly shaded eyes, must have left behind. And I saw him suddenly becoming aware of another presence in the room; looking up, possibly, with that faint smile still on his lips, to confront the brutish face and glowering eyes of his murderer.

And what had happened then? The man had suffocated him, so the police said. How had he ever got his hands on his throat before the utterance of the one outcry that would have brought help? There had been no such outcry. The thing had been done as silently as if it had been the work of evil spirits.

Try as I might, I could not construct a working hypothesis for those next few minutes. How had Pomeroy got in? How had he crossed the room and got into a position behind that swivel chair? For even if his victim had not had his eye on the door, that great mirror over there would have revealed him. Perhaps when the gallows had fairly overshadowed him, and the last hope of some technical means of escape had in fact gone, he might tell. Otherwise we should never know. We should know nothing more than that, at the end of those few horrible minutes they had opened the doctor's door and looked in, and, seeing his head and shoulders in silhouette against the window as he bent there over his desk, they thought him to be asleep or to have fainted.

And then, coming closer, close enough to see the terrible face and wild, glaring eyes, they knew he was dead by violence.

I shuddered uncontrollably, and wondered at my good spirits of so short a time before. I was glad Jack had gone. I could hardly have found the heart to give him so cheerfully confident a message to Madeline now.

Well, there was nothing to be gained by staying here, just to work up a wholly unnecessary attack of the horrors over the grewsome business.

I turned to go. Just as I did so, my eye caught a glint from the carpet, of what I took to be a bent pin. Quite automatically—for by nature I am an orderly and methodical person—I stooped and picked it up. It was not a pin after all, but the broken end of a curved needle. It made no particular impression on my mind, and I was on the point of dropping it into the waste-paper basket, when something stopped me. It was no very definite idea, probably just a reminiscence from detective stories I had read, of the immense importance of the most trivial things.

I smiled a little over my own action, but for all that, I put the needle back upon the exact spot on the carpet where I had found it, instead of tossing it among the crumpled papers in the basket.

My very last impression in that room was identical with my first one—how thoroughly it reeked of tobacco; what filthy brutes detectives were anyway.

I meant to walk down to my apartment off Madison Square, and, rather relishing the prospect of a quiet stroll under the warm spring night air, I took my time about starting, pulled on my gloves quite deliberately, and lighted a cigar in the sheltered entrance to the Grosvenor Building.

As I stood there, shielding my match with my hands, my walking stick tucked under my arm, I was somewhat startled by a touch on the elbow. Turning quickly, I saw the whispering man standing there.

"I wonder if I may trouble you for the rest of that match?" he asked. "I am in my chronic condition, amply provided with things to smoke and destitute of the means for setting them alight."

I offered him matches and waited until his cigar was drawing well, and then we went out in the street together.

"A thing like a murder seems strangely incongruous among all these commonplace, respectable surroundings," I observed.

"I don't know," said he. "I doubt if any time or any place is intrinsically better adapted to the crime of murder than the middle of the day, a crowded city street, and a modern office building. I was just wondering, as a matter of fact, why doctors and other professional men, who shut themselves up in private offices, aren't murdered oftener."

He was going south, too, it seemed, so we fell in step together, both rather glad, I think, to be able to talk to somebody without the need of making preliminary explanations. I was especially so, because there was something familiar about him, which baffled me because it was so vague. I was sure I had heard him talk before—in his natural voice, I mean, not in the horrible, croaking whisper which sometimes replaced it.

"You may be right in theory," said I. "I have a friend who would agree with you, but, as a practical matter of fact, this murderer has been overtaken and caught very promptly."

"Do you think so?" he asked. "If the police go on exhibiting the same plentiful lack of wit during the rest of the case which they have shown tonight in the Pomeroy affair, I should say the murderer had a good chance to die of old age."

I stopped dead-still in the middle of the sidewalk, and looked at him. "What do you mean?" I cried. "Do you mean to express a doubt that Pomeroy is the man who killed Dr. Marshall?"

"No doubt," said he quietly; "a certainty."

"And have you any objection to telling me on what you base that certainty?"

"None at all," said he. "It is very simple. You have no special knowledge of precious stones, I presume?"

"None whatever," I replied.

"Neither has that fool of a police lieutenant," was his rejoinder, "but I have; and I was able to see at a glance that the thing they found in

Pomeroy's pocket was no more a ruby than that big red vase in the drug-store window over there is. It was a clever imitation, I grant, but nothing more than that."

Mechanically I set my legs in motion again, and he walked on beside me in silence. It was impossible to doubt what he said; evidently he knew exactly what he was talking about.

"Still," said I, after a few minutes of quiet thought, "I don't see that the fact of its being an imitation clears Pomeroy as completely as you seem to think it does. It is not merely an imitation ruby, it is an imitation of Dr. Marshall's ruby, which makes it clear enough that the man intended to get the real one. We know he didn't succeed, but how do we know he didn't murder the doctor?"

"It's not very difficult, is it?" asked my companion politely. "If Pomeroy had contemplated the use of violence, he would hardly have gone to the trouble and run the risk of securing an imitation of the doctor's stone. What he meant to do is perfectly plain. He undoubtedly knew that Dr. Marshall frequently showed the ruby to his patients. If he, going in the guise of a patient, could persuade the doctor to show it to him, the robbery was as good as accomplished. It would only need a little clever sleight of hand, of which a man like Pomeroy is past master, to exchange the real one for the imitation. It might be weeks or months before the doctor would discover that any crime whatever had been committed, and when he did make that discovery he would have no way of knowing which of the patients to whom he had shown the stone was the criminal.

"It was a well-planned crime, and like every well-planned crime had this great merit: it did not commit the intending criminal to any criminal act until success was actually in his grasp. If the plan failed, if Pomeroy did not succeed in inducing the doctor to show him his stone, he lost no more than the cost of the imitation stone. Indeed, there would be nothing to prevent his going back for another trial whenever he pleased.

"Now I think you can see that no man in his senses—and a high-class crook like Pomeroy is certainly in full possession of his—with a safe, clever plan like that in his head, and the means for carrying it out in his skillful fingers, would wantonly have murdered the doctor and come away without his ruby."

I could see clearly enough that he was right. No man will do by violence what he is prepared to do, with better promise of success, by fraud.

"Why, then," I asked, "didn't Pomeroy wait his turn and go into the inner office in the character of a patient?"

"He was frightened away, I imagine," said my companion, "and I have a notion that I myself am the person who frightened him. I had mistaken him at first glance for someone I knew, and, catching his eye, I bowed to him, rather uncertainly, to be sure. But for all that, I think he believed I had recognized him. So he waited till I had gone into the doctor's office, and then slipped quietly away."

By that time we had got down to Twenty-sixth Street, and I must turn off across the square. But my vague, half recognition of the man troubled me, and I determined not to let him go without finding out who he was.

"I am wondering," said I, "if I have been similarly mistaken about you. It is your voice that sounds so familiar to me. I have no recollection of your face."

"That's natural enough," said he; "I am Carlton Stancliffe."

Carlton Stancliffe, of course. It was stupid of me not to have guessed, since I had put him down for an actor at my first glance at him. But it was no wonder that his face puzzled me, for his specialty was character parts, and, in the dozen times or more I must have seen him on the stage, he had never looked twice alike.

I told him my name, and expressed my pleasure at having met him. Then, rather thoughtlessly, I asked: "What are you playing in now, Mr. Stancliffe?"

He smiled rather sadly. "I should have spoken of myself in the past tense, I am afraid. With this nervous affection of the throat, I am as good as dead, though under Dr. Marshall's treatment I had hopes of a resurrection." Then, his mind going back to the grim topic we had for a moment forgotten, he murmured: "A peculiarly atrocious murder it must have been, but a very interesting one."

"Have you any theory regarding it," I asked, "now that Pomeroy is eliminated?"

He hesitated, "Why, yes," he said, "I have, but it's hardly one that I should care to talk about until it had turned out to be a good deal more than a theory."

I understood him well enough. I felt, as he spoke, the horrible black filaments of that sinister web of circumstances settling upon my spirits again.

"He's a singularly nice, clean-looking young chap, too," he added thoughtfully. Then, gravely, he bade me good night, and went on down the Avenue.

I was unlocking the door of my own apartment before it occurred to me to wonder a little over Mr. Stancliffe's last words. I had never seen Dr. Armstrong, but those words, somehow, did not seem like a description of him. They sounded more like a description of Jack. And where, anyway, had the actor seen the doctor's assistant?

I pulled the key out of the lock again, without turning it, and decided to knock on Jeffrey's door instead. I was wondering, in half-whimsical acquiescence in the claim he had put forth over the dinner table, what would have happened had he been able to spend the evening in my company. Would he have told the police to set Pomeroy free, and would his accusing finger have pointed at anyone else—at anyone I had seen and talked with since we had read the news together in the evening paper?

V

A Question of Minutes

Here and there in the memories of all of us are days which stand out of the dim past, bathed in a flood of light that spares us not a detail of them. Days like that may be called perpetual yesterdays. Such a day as that to me was the one that followed the murder of Dr. Marshall. It was the day of the coroner's inquest, and, from the moment I entered the big room in the Criminal Court building until the moment I left it, there was no relief from the strain of the most intense concentration to which I could key my mind, nor was there any respite from the rapid alternations between belief and incredulity, constantly recurring horror and intermittent relief.

And the worst shock of all, the most utterly and stupendously unexpected thing came as I was leaving the building, wearily telling myself that it was all over now at any rate. It was the sort of day I should not care to go through again.

I had warned Madeline, when she and Jack and I were riding downtown together to attend the inquest, that she would have to make up her mind to endure all the various discomforts of publicity which the ingenious minds of yellow city editors could subject her to. The Marshall affair was the biggest news of the day, and its participants must suffer the consequences. There would be lots of people waiting to stare at her, batteries of cameras to be faced, sketch artists and wiry young reporters of both sexes demanding interviews. These last she could, in a measure, be shielded from, but not from the others.

Of course, the arrest of Pomeroy and the events which had led up to it, and which had appeared in all the morning papers, would have, for a while at least, the effect of keeping the widow and her stepson out of the immediate center of the focus of attention.

They did not know yet how frail that barrier was and how soon it must give way. I had been in two minds whether to tell them of the astonishing fact which Mr. Stancliffe had so casually communicated to me the night before. My real reason, I suppose, was a cowardly and forlorn hope, which, since my conversation with Jeffrey, I had clung to, that perhaps Mr. Stancliffe did not know as much about precious stones as he thought he did. Jack had identified the ruby quite positively. Might he not be right in his identification after all? So long as there was a chance of it, I shrank from making them unnecessarily miserable.

As they were both wanted as witnesses, they did not go with me into the court room, but were ushered into a little anteroom adjoining, to wait until they should be called for.

The coroner took his seat. The jury filed in and took their places in the box. The oath was administered to them, and proceedings began.

If I had needed any further evidence that we were a celebrated case than was afforded by the presence of the crowd and the numerous reporters, I should have got it when I saw the district attorney himself elbowing his way brusquely down the aisle, and dropping into a seat just inside the railing. I knew Cromwell pretty well, and I was sure that unless he expected a larger share of notoriety than could be extracted from the conviction of an ordinary professional criminal in an ordinary case of robbery and murder, he would have manifested no such interest at this early stage of the proceedings.

The first witness called to the stand was the very blond young woman who had made the unsuccessful attempt to identify Pomeroy the night before. After she had given her name and address, and stated that she had been for several years in the employ of Dr. Marshall, the coroner framed his first important question.

"Please tell the jury, Miss Jerome, what the ordinary routine was in Dr. Marshall's office, and what your own particular duties were."

"The doctor," she said, "always received his patients in his own private office, which was in a corner of the building. They waited their turn to see him, out in the reception room where my desk was. I had to keep track of the order in which they came in, and to make a note of the ones who had special appointments with him. When he got through with a patient, he generally let them out, directly into the corridor without their coming back through the reception room."

"Could you hear, as a rule," the coroner asked, "when he opened the door and let a patient out?"

"No, sir, not unless the door was shut with a slam. The walls are specially deadened in that building, I think because it was intended for doctors and people like that, and the door was thick and fitted very closely."

"Tell the jury, then," continued the coroner, "how you knew when the doctor was through with one patient and ready to see another."

"Sometimes," she answered, "he used to open the door into the reception room and speak to me, but he only did that when he wanted to see how many patients were waiting for him. Generally he just gave two rings on his desk buzzer."

"Was there anything else you had to do?" the coroner asked.

"I had to answer the 'phone," said the girl. "When they were people the doctor wanted to talk to, I put them on his wire. When they weren't, I put them on Dr. Armstrong's. I had two plugs in the desk."

"Now," said the coroner, "to get down to the events of yesterday morning, was there anything which happened before twelve o'clock which struck you at all at the time, or which occurs to you now as you think back upon it, as out of the ordinary?"

For the first time in the course of her testimony, she hesitated a little. "I don't know that I would call it unusual," she said. "He got down a little late—ten minutes perhaps—and he seemed rather short-tempered, but he had been that for the last day or two."

"There was nothing else that caught your attention?"

"No, sir; nothing at all. There were a number of patients waiting to see him; just about the usual number I should say."

"Were you acquainted with most of them? Were they people who came frequently to see the doctor?"

"They were mostly strangers," she answered. "They usually were. People didn't come to see Dr. Marshall regularly. They got sent to him by other doctors. There were two or three who came in during the early part of the morning who were old patients. After 11 o'clock they were all strangers."

"So far as you know, they were strangers, that is."

"No; I am sure they were," the girl persisted.

"Do you mean to say," questioned the coroner, "that you were able to recognize at a glance everyone who has ever been a patient of Dr. Marshall's?"

"No, sir," said the girl. "But when a person comes in in a lost sort of way, not knowing which way to look, and then comes up to me and asks me if this is Dr. Marshall's office, I know that that person's a stranger."

"Very well," said the coroner, "who was the last person whom you admitted to Dr. Marshall's office?"

"She gave me her name," said the girl, "as Miss Gwendolen Carr, and said her address was the St. Anthony Hotel."

"Had she ever come to consult Dr. Marshall before?"

"No, sir. That was the first time I had ever seen her."

"Do you know what time it was when you admitted her to Dr. Marshall's office?"

"No, sir, I don't," she said. "I didn't happen to look at my watch until quite a long time afterwards."

"What time was it when you looked at your watch?"

"Ten minutes past twelve."

"And how long should you say it was then since Miss Carr had gone into the inner office?"

"I couldn't tell you."

"Give us your best judgment," persisted the coroner. "Was it an hour?"

"It may have been an hour, perhaps a little less."

"And what did you do then when you had looked at your watch?"

"I knew the doctor had an appointment at twelve o'clock, and that he considered it important, so I gave a short ring on his desk telephone."

"Did he answer the ring?"

"No, sir; he didn't unhook the receiver."

"Wasn't that rather extraordinary?"

"Oh, no, not at all. When he was very busy he never would answer the 'phone, unless I gave three rings. That meant it was important."

"You hadn't given three rings in this instance?"

"No, sir; one short one. And then I waited until half past twelve o'clock."

"Go on," said the coroner; "tell the jury, as plainly as you can, all that happened after that."

"Well," said the witness, "at half past twelve I thought I had better give three rings, because I knew his twelve o'clock appointment was important. I did, and listened at the 'phone to see if he wasn't going to answer. When he didn't, I rang again, and then all at once I began to wonder whether something wasn't the matter. So I got up from my desk and walked over to the door and opened it, and looked in. There was no one else there in the room. The doctor was sitting in his swivel chair at the farther side of his desk. I couldn't see his face very well, because the window was behind it, but he looked kind of funny somehow—not exactly natural, I mean. He was leaning forward in a queer way.

"For a minute I thought he had dropped asleep, and then I saw he hadn't. I don't know how I saw; I hadn't got very close. I turned round quick and went out into Dr. Armstrong's office."

"Did you go out into the corridor or go back through the reception room to get into Dr. Armstrong's office."

"I didn't have to do either. I went straight in. There's a door opening between."

"Was it locked?"

"No, sir. That door was never locked that I know of."

I believe every person in the room felt a little electrical thrill of premonition at that; certainly I did. I was reminded of what Madeline had said of the way everything fell into a pattern. Certainly that unlocked door was potentially suggestive.

"Well," said the coroner, "what did you tell Dr. Armstrong?"

"I didn't tell him anything. He wasn't there. By that time I was beginning to get a little frightened, and I went straight from his office out into the corridor, meaning to tell an elevator man to call some other doctor down from upstairs. I signaled the next car that was coming up, to stop, but when it stopped, I saw Dr. Armstrong getting out. He had a little package in his hand. I told him I was afraid something was wrong with the doctor, and I wanted him to go in and see."

"We went through the reception room. I made him go ahead, and I followed him back into Dr. Marshall's office."

"Tell, as fully as you can," said the coroner, "what conversation passed between you and Dr. Armstrong after you had gone through into the inner office."

"There wasn't much that you could call conversation," said the girl. "He was ahead of me, but when he got just about as far into the room as I had gotten the first time, he stopped and looked at—at what was sitting there humped over the desk, and he said 'My God!' in a kind of whisper, and then drew a long breath. Then he handed me the package he had with him and told me to go put it on his desk, and then come back. I did; it only took me about a quarter of a minute. When I got into the room again, he was leaning over the—the body and seemed to be feeling of the pulse. He said to me, 'Dr. Marshall is dead. I think he has had an attack of heart failure. You'd better go upstairs and call down Dr. Adams. As soon as you have done that, telephone for the police.'

"I did what he told me to. That was all. I didn't go back into the inner room where—it was."

It seemed to me that she had told her whole story, and I was a little surprised when the district attorney got up and asked permission to question her further. "You said, I believe," he began, "that the doctor's signal that he was ready to see another patient was two rings on his desk buzzer. Why was it two? What did one ring mean? Something else?"

"Yes, sir. It meant that I was to go into the office myself."

"Had he any other push buttons in his office besides the one which rang at your desk?"

"Yes, sir. There was one he used to call Dr. Armstrong."

"Both those buttons were on his desk?"

"Yes, sir."

"So that when he sat where he was when you found him, they would have been within easy reach of his hand?"

"Yes, sir."

"That's all," said the district attorney.

I felt a momentary surprise, not that these questions should be asked, but that they should be asked by the district attorney, for the import of them was plain enough. The answers they elicited weakened the case against Pomeroy tremendously; made it seem almost inconceivable that the doctor could have been slain by anyone toward whom he had entertained the slightest feeling of suspicion.

What troubled me about it was not the collapse of the case against Pomeroy; that I had foreseen, but I was sure Cromwell would not have set about demolishing it, unless he already had another and better one to put in its place. The evidence that told for Pomeroy must tell equally forcibly against someone else.

The very blond young woman left the stand, and her place was taken by the one I had heard designated by the police lieutenant last night as "the black-eyed one." I found myself experiencing a regret, which I fancy was shared by many of the other spectators, that we were likely to see her delicious face and hear her agreeable voice for so short a time. Her testimony, however important, would not take long to present.

She gave her name and the same address which she had confided to the telephone girl the day before, and then testified that on the day in question, from about ten o'clock in the morning, she had been waiting in Dr. Marshall's reception room for a chance to consult him.

"Were you personally acquainted with Dr. Marshall?" asked the coroner.

"No, sir. I had seen him. He had been pointed out to me from a distance, but I had never spoken to him."

"Your call upon him, then, was a professional one?"

"You mean, did I go to him as a patient? Yes, sir."

"Can you tell us, Miss Carr," the coroner asked, "what time it was when you were admitted to Dr. Marshall's inner office?"

"No, sir," she said, "I didn't happen to notice. I might be able to guess at it from the time it was when I went out."

"You know, then," asked the coroner eagerly, "what time it was when you did go out?"

"Yes, sir. I happened to glance up at the clock as I was walking toward the door—the door into the corridor, I mean. It was just twenty minutes to twelve."

"Where was the doctor when you left the office?"

"He was sitting in his chair behind his desk."

"He didn't walk over to the door with you?"

"No, sir."

"Was there anything," the coroner asked slowly—"anything that you may have observed at that time, or previously, to cause you to suspect anything unusual?" Then, as she did not answer at once, he framed the question again. "Did you notice any circumstance during your visit to Dr. Marshall's offices that struck you as suspicious, or strikes you so now, in the light of what is known to have happened afterwards?"

"No, sir," she said.

"You will realize, I think," said the coroner, "the extreme importance of the hour that you have testified to as that at which you left the office? That fixes the last moment when Dr. Marshall is known to have been alive. Have you any doubt whatever as to the accuracy of your memory?"

"I appreciate the importance of it," she said gravely, "but I am absolutely certain of the hour. It was twenty minutes before twelve when I happened to look up at the clock, just as I was opening the door from Dr. Marshall's office into the corridor."

VI

Dr. Armstrong Testifies

The coroner dismissed Gwendolen Carr from the stand, with the request that she remain at hand subject to call, as it might prove necessary to question her further at some later stage in the proceedings.

When the name of the next witness was called aloud, the perceptible stir it caused among the spectators testified to the rapidly rising interest. Dr. Walter Armstrong was the man who, according to the telephone girl's testimony, had had only an unlocked door between himself and his murdered employer.

I myself had never seen him before, and since my talk with Madeline of the night previous, was curious to do so. He made, I must confess, no very favorable impression upon me. His manner was didactic and self-satisfied, his gestures prim and angular. He was young—under thirty, I should say, but there was no suggestion of youthfulness, and nothing that seemed to mark the presence of the saving sense of humor. It occurred to me that if it were true that he had fallen a little in love with Madeline. Marshall, he would take himself very seriously. She had not said, to be sure, that he was, but she had pretty clearly suggested it.

The coroner began, almost immediately, to develop a highly suggestive line of inquiry. The moment the formal questions were out of the way, he said: "You're a specialist yourself, aren't you, Dr. Armstrong?"

"Yes, sir."

"As a matter of fact, aren't you a toxicologist—a student of poisons, in other words?"

"Of only a very limited group of poisons, sir," the doctor answered in his primly superior manner. "I have confined my studies to those vegetable alkaloids which act most directly upon the brain and the nerve centers."

He went on, under further questioning from the coroner, to outline the nature of his duties as Dr. Marshall's assistant. It appeared that they did not take all of his time, and that he had a considerable independent practice. He always kept the same office hours as Dr. Marshall, however, and was subject to call from him at any time. Many of the doctor's patients he simply turned over, after a single consultation, to his assistant.

"You say you were subject to call," observed the coroner. "Is it true that the doctor had a push button on his desk which served to summon you into his office?"

"Yes, sir."

"Did he call you at any time during yesterday morning?"

"Once or twice—yes, sir, but not after eleven o'clock, I think."

"He had every reason to believe that you were in the adjoining room, subject to call, as long as he remained in his office?"

"Yes, sir."

"How did it happen, Dr. Armstrong, that you were not in your office at half past twelve when Miss Jerome went in there to find you?"

"Dr. Marshall had an appointment at twelve o'clock," said the witness. "I knew it was important, and supposed he had gone to keep it. I did not hear him go out, but concluded that he must have done so, and went out on an errand myself."

"Do you know what time it was when you left your office?"

"Not exactly, no, sir."

"Did this errand of yours take you very far away?"

"Only to the instrument maker's on the first floor of our own building. I spent a good deal more time, however, than was necessary for the purpose of securing the article that I bought. The proprietor of the shop is a friend of mine."

The ensuing testimony merely corroborated that of Miss Jerome, the attendant in the reception room. She had met him at the elevator door, as she said, and they had gone together into the inner office. He had seen immediately that Dr. Marshall was dead, and had dispatched the girl in quest of Dr. Adams, whose office was on the floor above.

"Is it true," asked the coroner, "that you said to Miss Jerome, 'I think Dr. Marshall has had an attack of heart failure'?"

"I may have said something like that. I don't recall the words clearly now; don't remember speaking them at all, but the thought occurred to me."

"Had you any reason to anticipate a death of that sort for Dr. Marshall?"

"No, sir. He had been suffering from indigestion. An acute attack of that sort sometimes produces a mechanical effect on the heart which causes death."

"After mature reflection, do you still believe that that was the actual cause of death in this instance?"

"Mature reflection has nothing to do with the case," said the witness, with a touch of asperity. "It's a question of fact and can only be determined by examination. I was not present at the autopsy. I did not even make a careful examination of the body of the deceased. I did nothing beyond ascertaining that he was dead. Then I sent at once for a physician whose interest in the case was wholly professional."

"Do you think it possible," asked the coroner, unruffled by this outburst, "that the cause of death might have been suffocation, produced, say, by a hand held tightly over the mouth and nostrils of the deceased?"

"I should be unwilling," retorted the witness, "to state, as my professional opinion, that that was *not* the cause, for the reason that I am unwilling to state any professional opinion whatever."

Dr. Armstrong was temporarily excused from the stand at this point to make way for another witness, who had just arrived, and who was obviously in a hurry to get away again. I did not know who he was, until his first answers to the coroner's questions showed him to be the owner of the instrument shop on the first floor of the Grosvenor.

Yes, he knew Dr. Armstrong very well. The doctor had come into the shop a little after noon yesterday and made a little purchase, talked a while, and gone out again.

"Can you fix the time, with any degree of accuracy, when Dr. Armstrong came into your shop?"

"Yes, sir; it was sixteen minutes past twelve."

"You are quite sure of this?"

"Yes, sir. I had just looked at my watch and decided that it was time for me to go out to lunch, when I saw Dr. Armstrong coming in. I sold him what he wanted, and we talked for perhaps fifteen minutes."

"You say you had just looked at your watch. What assurance have you that your watch was right?"

"It runs right," said the instrument maker, with a certain amount of annoyance in his tone.

"Undoubtedly to your satisfaction," said the coroner. "It happens in this case, however, that the matter of time may well prove to be of the most vital importance. Can you corroborate the evidence offered by your watch in any way?"

"I had compared it at noon with the office clock," said the instrument maker.

"And is the office clock generally right?"

"It has to be right," said the witness.

"Please explain what you mean."

"It's an electric clock. It is connected on the same circuit with all the clocks in the building, and they are set every hour by telegraph from the observatory at Washington. All the clocks in that building are always right."

"Could one of them get out of order and stop?" asked the coroner.

"No, because they are all on one circuit. If one of them went wrong it would stop every clock in the whole building."

"That's all," said the coroner. But the district attorney wanted to ask a question.

"Dr. Armstrong talked to you in a perfectly natural, spontaneous way, did he?"

"Yes, sir."

"He did not seem to be laboring under any unusual excitement?"

"None at all, sir. I thought he looked a bit worried when I first caught sight of his face, but nothing more than that, sir."

"That's all."

The doctor then resumed the stand.

"You were in your office, Dr. Armstrong, from, say, eleven thirty until twelve fifteen?"

"If the latter hour is the time when I went out—yes, sir."

"Did you hear anything in Dr. Marshall's office to arouse your suspicion that all was not well there?"

"Nothing whatever."

"What might you have expected to hear from your position at your desk? Would an ordinary conversation in the doctor's office be audible?"

"No, sir."

"But if the voices were raised, as if in anger?"

"Then I think I should have heard them."

"If there had been a life-and-death struggle, such as a man of Dr. Marshall's physique could have made against an attempt to suffocate him, you would, in all human probability, have heard something of it?"

"I should be inclined to think so; yes, sir."

"And you heard nothing?"

"Nothing whatever."

"You are sure the doctor did not ring your bell?"

"Not after the last time I answered it."

"I think that's all for the present," said the coroner, "unless some member of the jury wishes to ask a question. Is there anything you wish to inquire about, gentlemen?"

There was a little silence after that. For my part my mind was centered on that blankly mysterious thirty-five minutes between twenty minutes to twelve, when Gwendolen Carr, if her testimony was to be believed, had left the doctor alive and well, sitting at his desk, and twelve fifteen, when his assistant had gone out of the adjoining office on his errand to the instrument maker's. Thirty-five minutes of silence. I felt again as I had felt the evening before when young Jack Marshall had inarticulately whispered "poison!" I seemed to read across the blank space of those thirty-five minutes the word "treachery" written in lurid letters.

I think the increasing tension of that moment, while we waited to see if any of the jury was going to act on the coroner's invitation, was felt by everyone in the room. I am sure the witness felt it, for I could see him turning a little pale and breathing a little quicker. But the tension was instantly relaxed when one of the jurors spoke up. He was a little ferret-faced man with a piping voice. "I'd like to know," he said, "what was in the package you brought back from the instrument maker's."

The utter irrelevance and futility of the question, asked, as it was, in that inquisitive piping voice, caused a sudden ripple of laughter in the room. Even the best behaved of us smiled, and the coroner himself, though he sternly commanded silence, was not able to extinguish the twinkle in his eye when he repeated the question.

But the assistant showed no inclination to laugh; nor, on the other hand, did he resent the question as an impertinence. He answered, in fact, rather gravely, "What I bought was a new hypodermic syringe. The one I had been using had a fall and the needle was broken. That is a very necessary instrument to a man in my profession. So I went down to the instrument maker's, as soon as I could, and bought a new one."

They summoned other witnesses after that, witnesses whose testimony was far more sensational from the point of view of other spectators at the inquest than anything that had gone before. Pomeroy, the professional crook, against whom the case had seemed last night so perfect, was able to prove a positive alibi; and Dr. Marshall's jeweler testified that the supposed ruby which the police had found in Pomeroy's pocket was nothing but an imitation. The true ruby was undisturbed in the doctor's safe.

It must have been very dramatic, this sudden collapse of the theory of the crime which everybody present, except, perhaps, the coroner, the district attorney, and myself, had unhesitatingly accepted. But I sat there through it all, wholly unconscious of the rising excitement, of the swiftly interchanged looks, the buzz of whispered conversation, the dawning in every face of some new and much more terrible surmise. It was not because this result had been a foregone conclusion to me that I remained thus oblivious to my surroundings. It was because the whole of my thinking power was focused on something else; upon the small curved, gleaming bit of steel which I had first mistaken for a bent pin upon the carpet in Dr. Marshall's inner office. The thing I had picked up, and then laughed at myself for replacing where I had seen it. I knew what it was now. It was the broken end of a hollow hypodermic needle.

VII

The Balance of Probability

Jack, dear, do try to cheer up and eat something. The world isn't coming to an end, and no innocent person is going to suffer for your father's murder. Cliff here will attend to that. You and I are innocent, and I believe Dr. Armstrong is. I believe it just as much as I did this morning, though of course it was plain what Mr. Cromwell was getting at. There are going to be hard times for all of us until it is cleared up, but it will be cleared up in the end. Come, eat that sweatbread; it's delicious. And try to smile a little."

We were lunching, not, indeed, where I could have wished to take them, but in the least impossible place that was near at hand. The coroner had adjourned the inquest for only an hour, which put going uptown out of the question.

Madeline had endured the strain and the discomfort of the morning with a calmness which was hard for me to understand, and with a courage that I found it difficult to admire sufficiently. She needed an extra supply to compensate for her stepson's weakness. He had yielded, only after a good deal of resistance, to my suggestion that we go out to lunch, and had made almost no pretense at eating anything.

The more I watched this young man, the less I could understand him. He had never impressed me as one likely to turn weak in a crisis, and yet he seemed to be deplorably so. Madeline had said there would be hard times for all of them, and that was a mild way of putting it if the evidence were to go on developing in the direction it had taken against Dr. Armstrong. But it would be infinitely harder for Madeline than for Jack. Her name was sure to be coupled with that of the suspected doctor in a way that, at the best, would be disagreeable, and at the worst would be unthinkably distressing. If his guilt were proved, her own innocence could hardly remain unquestioned.

It was clear enough in this circumstance that Jack should have risen to the situation; should have encouraged her, rather than leaned upon her for support himself.

Just as we were about to leave the restaurant, a little incident happened which I must mention here, although it seemed insignificant enough at the time. The brief hour which the coroner had allowed us for recess had almost passed, and we were in the act of rising from our table, when behind me I heard a chair move back, and the next moment, somewhat to my surprise, my friend Jeffrey walked round our table and went straight up to Madeline. What he said to her amounted to nothing, except for what was omitted.

He said nothing whatever by way of condolence over Dr. Marshall's death, but spoke merely of the course of events of the inquest, which it appeared he had attended, and attempted to cheer her with the thought that it would soon be over.

It suddenly occurred to me while he talked that he must have seen her since her husband's death. It was only last evening at dinner time that we had got the news of it. He would hardly have called at the house, let alone been admitted to see her last evening while Jack and I were down at the Grosvenor, unless there were between them a much greater degree of intimacy than he had allowed me to suppose. Then, too, it seemed that while she stood talking to him there her color was a little higher, her eyes brighter; that there was less of the calm, cold restraint in her manner than there had been before.

We left him to go back to his unfinished lunch, and drove back, rather silently, to the Criminal Courts building. I was feeling rather annoyed, but with myself rather than with Madeline, for attaching what I assured myself was an altogether exaggerated importance to the little incident of our meeting with Jeffrey.

What Jack was thinking about I could not guess. He had paid very little attention to Jeffrey; had hardly spoken to him at all, unless I was mistaken. He seemed entirely engrossed with a train of thought that was all his own. I knew he would be called as a witness, and rather dreaded his appearance on the stand.

It was nearly half an hour after the time set by the coroner for the continuation of the inquest before that functionary, accompanied by the district attorney and a third man, whom I did not recognize, emerged from the private office. The district attorney and the stranger seated themselves within the railed-in space and continued a low-voiced conversation.

The coroner, as soon as the room had been brought to order, summoned the first witness for the afternoon, John Roscoe Marshall. He had had a junior after that name until yesterday.

He answered the formal routine questions with which his testimony was inaugurated in a rather listless manner, which told me that the mysterious something, whatever it was, that had occupied his mind during the lunch hour was still dominant in his thoughts.

It was not long before the coroner roused his full attention. "You saw your father, Mr. Marshall, yesterday morning before he went downtown to his office?"

"Yes, sir."

"Did you see him for more than a moment?"

"Yes, sir, we breakfasted together. We had some conversation."

The coroner leaned forward as he asked the next question. "Did you happen to observe whether or not, at that time, there was any sort of wound or scratch upon your father's throat, or anything that might have been such a wound or scratch, but was covered by a piece of adhesive surgical plaster?"

"No, sir," said the witness in some surprise, "there was nothing of the sort there."

"You mean, I suppose," continued the coroner, "that you happened to notice nothing of the sort there?"

"No, sir, I meant there *was* nothing. My father had a habit in conversation, especially when he was a trifle excited, of putting back his head and thrusting out his chin in such a way as to get the edge of his beard clear from his collar. I noticed particularly his doing that yesterday morning, and I am sure there was nothing of the sort you speak of above the line of the collar."

"That's all, Mr. Marshall," said the coroner.

Jack looked at him in astonishment. "You mean you are through with me?" he asked.

"For the present. I may wish to recall you to the stand later. You may step down now."

Madeline was called to the stand immediately afterwards, and, to my increasing surprise, she was asked exactly the same questions we had just heard her stepson answer. Her answers were the same as his, or practically so. And then she, too, was excused, though with the provision that she might be recalled.

The question had already begun to take on a sort of uncanny force just from its apparent triviality and the number of times it was insisted upon. This effect was increased still further when Gwendolen Carr was recalled to the stand, only to have the same question, for a third time, asked of her.

"Before twenty minutes to twelve, Miss Carr, when you left Dr. Marshall's office, was there such a wound or any such bit of surgical plaster, as you have just heard me describe, on Dr. Marshall's throat?"

"No, sir."

"You are quite sure?"

"Quite sure."

Almost before she had got the words uttered, a sudden look of alarm, almost of terror, in her eyes attracted my attention. She seemed to be looking straight at Jack, who, after leaving the stand, had taken a seat beside me. I followed her gaze quickly enough to see him sway where he sat, but not in time to save him from falling out of his chair in a dead faint.

He recovered quickly in the cool fresh air of the corridor, whither we carried him, and the coroner sent out word that he might go home, as it would probably not be necessary to call on him for any further testimony.

I found myself a little puzzled to account for the expression of alarm I had seen for a moment in Gwendolen Carr's face. It seemed sharper and more poignant than the mere sight of a fainting man would suffice to explain.

But the testimony of the next witness effectually diverted my mind from any such fine-spun speculations as that. He was the stranger who had come out of the coroner's office accompanied by that official and the district attorney. He now proved to be the coroner's physician, who had conducted the autopsy on the body of the murdered man.

"State what, in your opinion, was the cause of the death." This was the question I heard the coroner asking when I reëntered the room.

"The cause of death was instantaneous collapse accompanying paralysis of the heart and of the organs of respiration. This was due to the presence, in a quantity sufficient to produce a toxic effect, of some unidentified vegetable alkaloid."

"In other words," said the coroner, "in your opinion, the deceased met his death by poison?"

"Yes, sir, beyond a doubt."

"What was that poison?"

"That is a question," replied the doctor slowly, "which at present I am unable to answer. The process of chemical analysis is one of elimination. There are a great many poisons which we are quite sure this is not, but we have not been able yet to determine absolutely what it is."

"You are quite sure, then, that it is not one of the commoner poisons?"

"Yes, sir. It is a poison which I never encountered before in my experience. By its action it must be of a singularly deadly nature. In this case I am sure that death ensued practically instantaneously after its administration."

"Have you been able to determine," asked the coroner, "in what manner it was administered?"

"Yes, sir. The stomach showed no trace of it whatever. It was injected hypodermically, probably by means of a hypodermic syringe. I found a puncture in the throat extending through the sternomastoid muscle into the left internal jugular, which undoubtedly was the channel by which the poison was injected into the body. The very small wound in the skin was sealed up by means of a small piece of adhesive surgical plaster."

"In your opinion," inquired the coroner, "is it possible that this poison was administered by the hand of the deceased himself?"

"No, sir, for three reasons. First, the direction of the stroke itself makes it almost impossible that it could have been delivered by the hand of the deceased. Second, death must have ensued, as the result of the poison, before it would have been possible to seal up the external wound in the manner I have described. Third, the syringe which contained the poison was not found upon or near the doctor's person."

"So there is no doubt whatever in your mind that the poison was administered to Dr. Marshall by another hand than his own?"

"No doubt whatever, sir."

There was a little period of silence after that. A good many of the spectators, and I must include myself among the number, turned involuntarily to look at the rigidly erect figure and the pale, twitching face of the man Armstrong, against whom so terrible a mountain of suspicion seemed to be piling up. He seemed unconscious of this concentrated gaze, and kept his bright, spectacled eyes directed fixedly upon the witness.

"In your opinion, Dr. Schmidt," the coroner asked at the end of the little silence—"in your opinion, was any purpose served by injecting this poison directly into the jugular vein?"

"Yes, sir. This is an immense vein leading directly to the heart, which is the organ upon which the poison seems to have acted primarily. Its effect would be very much quicker for being thus administered. In this case it must have been, as I said, instantaneous. The victim could hardly have had time to utter a cry."

"Speaking as a physician, should you say that it was an easy matter to reach the vein you speak of with a single stroke of a hypodermic needle?"

The little German doctor on the stand shook his head vehemently. "On the contrary, sir," he said, "it was, from a surgical point of view, an operation of the extremest nicety. The sternomastoid muscle through which the needle had to pass is a broad heavy band, which would present no landmark to the operator for the vein he sought."

"By 'the operator' you mean the murderer? "questioned the coroner.

"That is what I mean," assented the witness, "but I find myself compelled to regard it, from a technical point of view, as a surgical operation. I think it would be difficult for any of my profession to think of it in any other terms, or to regard it without a considerable degree of admiration."

"You would be inclined, then, to attribute the act to some member of your profession?"

"Not only that, but to a very clever one," said the witness, "unless, of course, the blow was struck under no other direction than that of blind chance. It might happen once in a thousand times that a blow so directed, with such an instrument, would find that vein. We have, of course, no means of knowing that this is not the one time out of a thousand, but the balance of probability is enormously against it. I may say, also, that the employment of a poison of so rare and unusual a nature as to baffle, so far, all our attempts to analyze it points very strongly in the same direction."

The coroner had one more question to ask. "Would it have been possible, in your opinion, Dr. Schmidt, for the operation to have been performed against the serious resistance of the deceased?"

"It could only have been done in one of two ways," the witness answered very gravely. "The direction of the stroke was downward. To have delivered it, the operator must have been able to come very close to his victim, either standing behind him, or reclining himself, with Dr. Marshall bending over him. He must have been able to touch the throat with his fingers without exciting suspicion. The slightest resistance, such as would have resulted from the faintest guess as to his intention, would have frustrated the attempt absolutely."

The coroner did not call the next witness immediately. He sat there at his desk, a little envelope in his hand, and although his eyes were lowered, he did not appear to be looking at it.

I glanced over toward the jury. They sat there, every man of them, with the same curious fixed look about their faces that I had seen in the coroner's. No one of them was looking in Walter Armstrong's direction.

Their horror at the deed he had done—the deed he must have done, that no one else could have had the opportunity to do—seemed to make it impossible for them to look at him.

Who else but he could be the criminal? Who else could have got into that room without exciting the victim's suspicion? Who else than this admitted student of poisons would have filled his syringe with a drug so rare that it baffled the chemists? Who but a clever surgeon could have directed his needle point into that broad avenue that led so instantly to the heart?

But there was more to come. This mountain of suspicion was to be piled higher yet, until it reached the altitude of utter certainty.

Already the coroner was calling the next witness. "Thomas Mealy."

VIII

What Jack Marshall Knew

The man who took the stand in response to this summons I recognized instantly as the young police officer who had been left in charge of the scene of the crime the night before. He sat very squarely on the witness chair, his helmet on his knees, his face composed into a perfectly meaningless official expression which members of the force nearly always exhibit when they are on the stand.

After the routine questions, which served to inform the jury who he was and what his connection with the case amounted to, the coroner handed him the envelope which he had been holding in his fingers. "Open that," he said, "and tell me if you know what the object is that it contains."

"No, sorr, I don't."

"Do you recognize it?"

"D'you mean, have I iver seen it before? Yes, sorr."

"Tell the jury where it was when you saw it."

"It was last evenin', late, after the lootenant and the rest of thim had gone away, I was lookin' about, not thinkin' of much of anythin', when I saw somethin' shinin' on the carpet. It looked like steel, and it was stickin' up like, so that I was afraid I might step on it and get it in my feet as I was walkin' about. I picked it up, and this was it, sorr."

"You are quite sure that was the thing you picked up?"

"Yes, sorr."

"Tell us exactly where it was when you saw it."

"Why, it was on the carpet, sorr, in Dr. Marshall's inner office, two or three paces away from the desk, I should say."

"What did you do with it when you picked it up?"

"I stuck it in this little envelope and put it in my pocket, and this mornin' I showed it to the inspector."

The witness was excused, after having handed back to the coroner the envelope and the thing it contained. Then, very gravely, the coroner looked down at the man who was sitting within arm's reach of me. "I am afraid I must call you to the stand again, Dr. Armstrong," he said.

The new witness rose and walked steadily up to the chair on the witness stand. He was very pale, but he did not look terror-stricken or guilty. He faced his inquisitor without flinching.

The coroner handed the envelope to him. "Can you tell the jury what that object is, Dr. Armstrong?"

The young doctor took the curved bit of steel, looked at it closely, appeared, somewhat to my surprise, to smell of it, and then seemed to let his mind glide off into a sort of reverie, unconscious of the fact that we were all waiting for his answer to the question.

The coroner repeated it rather sharply. "Do you know what it is, Dr. Armstrong?"

He came back to his present surroundings with a start. "Yes, sir," he said. "It is the broken end of a hypodermic needle."

"In your testimony this morning, Dr. Armstrong, you mentioned the fact that your own hypodermic needle was broken yesterday morning. You may recall this statement as the reason you alleged for your errand to the instrument shop on the first floor. Dr. Armstrong, was that needle which you hold in your fingers broken from the end of your own hypodermic syringe?"

"No, sir," said the doctor quietly.

The question might as well have been, "Are you the man who murdered Dr. Marshall?" But there was no vehemence, no suggestion of protest in the tone of the witness's voice.

"Are you able," the coroner continued, "to produce the broken point of your own needle?"

"No, sir. It fell from my hand while I was washing it, and the broken end went down the drain."

Well, the chain was complete at last. On the witness's own testimony, he had sat alone in a room, with direct access to the murdered man, at the time when the murder was committed. The instrument of death had been a hypodermic syringe, which had been broken in the encounter. And again returning to the testimony of the witness himself, this man who sat there now in the witness box had gone out to purchase a new, similar instrument within an hour of the commission of the murder.

The witness seemed to realize how perfectly the links of the chain fitted together, but something, either the incandescent clarity of his innocence or the most stupendous, impudent effrontery, was sustaining him.

He seemed loath to hand the needle point back to the coroner. He took off his spectacles for a better look at it; rubbed his finger along its curved surface. The coroner was holding out his hand, waiting to take it back, when the witness met his look, and it was the witness who asked the next question.

"Is it your theory, sir, that this needle was the one used by the murderer?"

"You are on the stand to answer questions, not to ask them."

But the witness proceeded, unabashed: "I believe that is your theory. If it is, and if it's right, I think I can provide the coroner's physician with a hint as to the nature of the poison used. I believe that I recognize it."

I think it is safe to say that everyone in that room who heard his words gasped with astonishment. Here was innocence or effrontery with a vengeance, and for the moment I think most of our minds inclined toward the latter.

There was a moment of dead silence. Then the coroner said, rather hoarsely: "Go on, sir. You may tell us your belief in the matter."

"I think," said the witness, "that the liquid which was driven through this needle was a powerful solution of nicotine bitartrate. It is one of the essential principles of the tobacco plant, and one of the deadliest and swiftest known poisons. Of course it would require a chemical analysis to prove the correctness of my opinion, but I myself have very little doubt of it."

"Did you ever hear of a case, doctor"—it was the coroner who spoke—"of this poison being used upon a human being?"

"Such cases are rare," the witness answered promptly, "but some few are known. I know of only one murder in which this was the poison used."

"But you do know of one?"

"Yes, sir. A certain French count, whose name at the moment escapes me, was murdered by means of this poison somewhere back in the eighties."

"Have you at present in your laboratory any sample of this poison, Dr. Armstrong?"

"I think so, sir. I am not sure. For that matter, it occurs in the American Pharmacopoeia. Any doctor can get it."

Strange as it may seem, I think the effect of the doctor's candor with the coroner, myself, the jury, and the spectators told against rather than for him. It produced so strong and instantaneous an impression of innocence that the mind reacted from it, and reflected that this impression was just exactly what it had been calculated to produce.

The coroner had no more questions to ask, neither had any member of the jury, but the district attorney was on his feet, asking for a word more.

I think that had it not been for the effect that might be produced on the jury by the amazing information which Dr. Armstrong had volunteered, Cromwell would have spared the witness these last twists of the thumbscrews. But he was quite merciless and meant to take no chances.

"Is it true, Dr. Armstrong," he asked, "that just before the murder you were on the point of severing your connection with Dr. Marshall and leaving the city?"

That shot told plainly enough. The witness started, his hands clenched convulsively on the chair arm, and he pressed his lips tight together for a moment before he attempted to answer. Finally he nodded his head, and contrived to utter the word "Yes."

"Is it also true," his inquisitor went on, "that you had quarreled with the deceased, and that your decision to go away was the result of this quarrel?"

"Partly; yes, sir."

"You had been on very friendly terms with him previously, had you not; not only with him, with his—family?"

"Yes, that is true."

"You had been a frequent visitor at his house, had you not?"

"Yes, sir."

The district attorney, with a grim smile on his pugnacious face, turned sharply away with a little shrug of his shoulders, and he let fifteen or twenty seconds intervene before he asked the next question. When he did ask it, he contrived to get into his inflection of the words the suggestion that asking it was a mere form of law, and that it was impossible there should be an answer.

"Do you care to state to the jury the cause of your quarrel with Dr. Marshall?" he asked.

"No," said the witness, between his white lips. "That's quite impossible."

"That's enough," said the district attorney.

The coroner's summing up of the case and the retirement of the jury to deliberate was a mere matter of form. They could have reached their verdict without leaving their seats, as far as that went.

Dr. Armstrong betrayed neither fear nor excitement when he heard the verdict. It had been practically a foregone conclusion all the afternoon, and he was ready for it.

He listened without a quiver to the words which deprived him of his liberty, turned to the nearest officer and said:

"Take me across the bridge. I am ready."

The formalities were few and swift.

In the crowd of spectators I drifted out of the room and down the corridor. I was wondering how it happened that, after all, now that it was over, the chain of testimony which the inquest had brought out complete in every detail, providing the motive, the opportunity, and the method of the murder, and pointing it all straight at one man, still failed to produce in me a full and satisfactory conviction of his guilt. And then came the thought, which I mentioned at the beginning of my account of the day's proceedings, that at any rate it was all over, at least for today. Until a night's sleep and a little leisure for quiet reflection should have brought back a clear mind again, there could be nothing more to grapple with. But there I was mistaken.

It was late in the afternoon and the corridor was not very well lighted, but for all that I was able to recognize the figure of the man who stood back in the shadowy angle of it watching the stream of spectators that was drifting out. He was the man who had fainted and whom the coroner had excused from further attendance on the inquest—my young friend, Jack Marshall.

It only needed one look at his face to convince me that the perplexities and surprises of my day were not exhausted yet, for if the wildly staring eyes of the man who now clutched my arm were prophets of the truth, something was going to happen at once.

"Come with me!" he gasped hoarsely. "I've got something to say to you!"

The hand which clutched my arm in a convulsive grasp was trembling uncontrollably.

"Steady," said I. "There is plenty of time. Walk along quietly with me until we are out of the crowd."

We turned down White Street, crossed Baxter, and went into Mulberry Bend Park. It was the late afternoon of a warm spring day, and the little park teemed and swarmed with humanity. But it was the sort of humanity that would have no ears for our conversation.

"Sit down here, now," said I, "and tell me what you have to say."

He began with a question. "Have they held Armstrong?"

I nodded. "He's locked up in the Tombs already," said I.

"Drew," the young man whispered, "he didn't do it. *He didn't do it!*"

"I wish I could be sure," said I. "Of course, the circumstances seem to establish an almost irresistible case against him. I think that any jury would find him guilty on the evidence that has been developed at the inquest today, and yet somehow I can't find it in my heart to believe he did it."

"That's not my trouble," said Jack. "I wish to Heaven I could believe he did it. I don't know how much I would give—my life, I think—to be able to believe that it was Dr. Armstrong who murdered my father, but I can't; because, Drew, I know he didn't. I *know* he didn't. He hadn't any chance to do it."

"Then," said I, trying in vain to speak steadily, "if you know that, you know more than the coroner knows. You know something that ought to have come out at the inquest today. As a result of that inquest, if your knowledge is correct—if there is no possibility of mistake about it—then an innocent man is locked in a cell over there in the Tombs prison. We shall have to have the truth now, Jack, whoever it hurts, whatever the consequences may be. But can you be sure, absolutely sure, that Dr. Armstrong was innocent after all?"

"Yes," he said, "that's the one thing I can be sure of. He was down at the instrument maker's, wasn't he, from a quarter past twelve till half past twelve?"

"Yes," said I. "What of that?"

He was shuddering so that he could scarcely speak, but he finally compelled the words to his trembling lips:

"This is what I know," he said. "I know that someone came out of my father's office at twenty minutes past twelve. I know who that person was."

There was a moment of silence while I waited for him to speak the name, but it soon became evident that he did not mean to do it.

"Who was it, Jack?" I asked. "You must tell me that now, whoever it was."

"Not yet," he said with a sort of gasp; "I must see her first. I must try again to get her to tell me the truth!"

IX

The Last Patient

I must try again to get her to tell me the truth."

The words fell like lead upon my mind, and left me half stunned with horror. Before I could utter a word he spoke again.

"Don't ask me any more questions. Don't try to find out, and don't follow me. I am going to see her now."

He sprang up from his seat on the bench before he had finished speaking, and without giving me time for a word of protest he rushed away across the park.

I did not attempt to follow him. I was, in fact, incapable of doing so. I sank back upon my bench and closed my eyes, trying to steady the world that was reeling round me. How long I sat there I do not know; probably for the better part of an hour. Then, summoning all my resolution, I got up and walked slowly back to the Worth Street station in the Subway, and there took a train uptown.

There was no doubt about my destination. There was only one place where I could go. Before I should see or talk with anyone else, before I dared allow my thought even to follow the suspicions which Jack Marshall's hard words had reawakened, I must see Madeline myself again and talk with her.

She received me after a little delay in the same room—the big, dim library—whither Jack had conducted me for the first time a little less than twenty-four hours ago. She wore the same lavender-colored house frock she had worn on that occasion. But this time when she entered she did not go over to the wall switch and flood the room with light. She sank rather wearily into a big chair and motioned me into another at the other side of the hearth.

"Madeline—" said I.

She interrupted me. "Let me say something first. I am glad you have come. I hope you will stay to dinner. It seems good to have you here somehow, but please let's not talk about anything that concerns these last two dreadful days. Let's talk about old times."

Her words made my task ten times harder. I rose miserably to my feet.

"Has Jack come home?" I asked.

"I think not," she said. "At least I have not seen him. I missed you as I came out from the inquest, and when I turned to look for you I thought I saw you going off with him."

"You did," said I, "but he left me abruptly and I thought he meant to come straight home."

There was a little silence after that. She waited for me to speak, and finally I began.

"Madeline," said I, "I wish with all my heart that we could do as you say—forget for a while these dreadful days and talk about old times—but there is something else that must come first. Before Jack left me this afternoon he told me something that did not come out at the inquest, and I must, I *must* talk to you about it. I have no alternative."

She sighed wearily. "Very well, then," she said.

"Jack told me," I began, "that Dr. Armstrong is innocent."

"Well, I think so, too," she said. "My belief in that was not shaken by the inquest at least. I am glad Jack agrees with me."

"Jack is not glad," said I gravely. "He's in despair. He told me that he would give anything—his life, he thought—to be rid of the knowledge that convinces him that Dr. Armstrong is innocent."

She started and looked at me intently.

"What do you mean?" she asked.

"Jack knows," I went on, looking at her intently, "Jack knows who it was who came out of Dr. Marshall's office at twenty minutes past twelve on the day of the murder. It was a woman."

Madeline dropped back rather limply in her chair.

"Oh, the poor, poor boy," she said, half under her breath. Then she asked me a question: "Did Jack tell you who it was that he saw?"

"No," said I. "He said he meant to see her again and try to get her to tell the truth."

The expression in Madeline's face hardened suddenly. "And you think," she observed, a world of scornful anger in her voice, "you think it was I who came out of the office at that hour."

"I have not said so," I protested; "I have accused you of nothing."

"Don't quibble," she said. "As a matter of fact, you did say you suspected me, though you didn't mean to. You said just now that Jack left you to see the woman and to try to get her to tell the truth, and you said five minutes ago that you suspected he had come straight home. That makes it clear enough, I think, what you are thinking of. I am not sure that you really deserve an answer, but I will make you one. I did not come out of Dr. Marshall's office at twenty minutes past twelve or at any other time on the day of the murder, for the simple reason that I didn't go into it on that day."

"Well," said I gravely, "I am very, very glad. I did think from the way Jack spoke that it was you he saw, and I think in time you will forgive me for having thought so natural a thing."

"Oh, I forgive you now," she said halfheartedly, "but I find it a little difficult. I suppose I should not blame my friends for having suspected me of having murdered my husband, when the circumstances really point in that direction. But I think I have a right to expect that they use a little ordinary reason in the matter. Why, Clifford Drew, do you suppose after all the evidence at the inquest that Jack would feel that Dr. Armstrong's innocence was established beyond a doubt by the fact that *I* came out of the doctor's office at twenty minutes past twelve? Wouldn't that implicate him all the more deeply, if anything?"

The sudden truth of what she said left me speechless. I was seven times a fool not to have seen it when I sat there in the park; seen it and rejoiced instead of dolefully imagining that the world was coming to an end.

"Come, don't worry about it," she said at length. "You meant all right, and we are all so tired and so dazed that we are hardly responsible. But poor, poor Jack!"

"Do you know who it was he saw?" I asked.

"No, I don't know."

"But you can guess?"

"I could make a guess that might or might not be right, but I don't mean to do it."

"Well," said I, "I feel that I must do something. The position of leaving an innocent man locked up in the Tombs under the weight of such an appalling amount of circumstantial evidence as has been piled upon Dr. Armstrong, is intolerable."

"I shan't say another word about it," she said positively. "If you want to accept the terms I first proposed when I came down to see you, and sit here quietly till Jack comes home, you may; otherwise I shall have to ask you to go. When Jack comes in he will probably be able to clear everything up. As for Dr. Armstrong, I don't think he will mind spending an evening or even a day or two in a nice comfortable cell where he can't be pestered. I wish I were in one myself."

I accepted her terms somewhat sulkily. But even when they were accepted, the subject of conversation didn't get very far away from the dreadful mystery that enveloped us. We got farthest away from it when she told me the story of the man whom Dr. Marshall had ruined years ago, just as he had meant to ruin this man now.

I meant to stay until Jack came home, but when the big hall clock struck eight I gave it up. He might have gone to my rooms anyway, and be waiting for me there. In case he came home at any reasonable hour I left word that I was to be telephoned for.

I picked up a hasty dinner in a restaurant on the way down to the Atlas, and, arriving there, went straight to Jeffrey's rooms. I opened my own door into the corridor and left it ajar, so that I could hear the telephone when it rang. Then I settled down to talk it out with Jeffrey. In the web of perplexity in which I was then involved, it was a downright necessity to me to talk over the whole affair with someone in whom I could place implicit confidence.

There was a good deal that I wanted to say, wanted him to hear, and I had talked for some time before I began gradually to become aware that he was unusually silent, if not absolutely indifferent.

"After all, she was quite tired out," he said at last, after I had described at some length my unsatisfactory interview with Madeline. "Anyway, so far as I can see, she gave you all you had a right to ask for, in the assurance that she didn't know whom Jack meant by 'her.' If you pressed her for more than that, I don't wonder she quarreled with you."

"Oh, we didn't quarrel exactly, but I think she might have tried to help. Certainly she could have offered some suggestion. She has known that boy very well in the last two years, better in many ways than his own mother could have known him, and she must have been able to offer some hint."

"Not necessarily; and even though she could, what good would a hint do, and what harm is done by waiting? Oh, I know an innocent man will spend the night in the Tombs, but there are plenty more innocent men in there to keep him company, and plenty of guilty ones outside for company to the murderer, whoever he is."

"It's all very well for you to take that detached view of it," said I, "because it doesn't matter a tallow dip to you, one way or the other. But I happen to care. I have too much regard for Madeline herself to feel comfortable leaving her under suspicion that way."

"Leaving who under suspicion?" Jeffrey demanded. Then, as I was too much surprised by the open anger in his voice to answer immediately, he went on: "Why, you silly ass, do you mean that you suspect that Madeline Marshall was the person who came out of that office at twelve twenty?"

"On the contrary, I am convinced she was not," said I stiffly, for his manner had really been offensive. "But no one of ordinary intelligence could help seeing that suspicion will attach to her until Dr. Armstrong is cleared."

"No one with a grain of imagination who had ever looked her straight in the face would entertain such a suspicion. You seem to think you are living in the days of the early Italian Renaissance. You'd better go to bed and sleep it off."

He tried to say it with an air of good humor and banter, but was powerless to disguise the fact that he was both in earnest and angry. Even if I haven't much imagination, I could see that.

And I happened to see something else, too—something that a man, who cared as little for appearances as he professed to, would hardly have tried to hide. There was a note on his table, of which only a corner of the envelope was visible, projecting out from under a folded evening paper that had been laid down over it. I happened to brush against the table as I was leaving the room, and the note fell to the floor. It was exactly at my feet, so I stooped to pick it up, in spite of the "Never mind" which Jeffrey uttered casually enough when he saw what had happened. The note was addressed to Jeffrey, and it was in Madeline Marshall's handwriting.

I went across to my own apartment, shut the door behind me, and sat down to think. "Why, why," I asked myself, "need this black web of suspicion and mystery spread itself over one after another of my friends?" That it should include Jack and Madeline was bad enough, but when it stretched to cover Arthur Jeffrey, too—this was the last straw. There was absolutely nothing tangible against him, of course. It was nothing that he had received a note from Madeline—I shouldn't want to be suspected on similar grounds myself—but he had deliberately kept me in the dark, was still keeping me in the dark, and I felt that he had become impossible as a confidant until he should be willing to give me his confidence too.

And I did want somebody to tell my story to. It would clarify itself just in the telling, I felt sure.

The thought of the actor, Carlton Stancliffe, had occurred to me a good many times during the day. I recalled his interest in the case, the valuable hint he had given me as to the counterfeit nature of Pomeroy's ruby, and remembered that he had admitted having a theory of his own for the case.

On the impulse of the moment, I looked up his address on the card he had given me, and called him over the telephone. My call was answered, and I had asked that Mr. Stancliffe be summoned to the 'phone, before the inconsiderateness of the act occurred to me. Of course, without a voice, he could hardly be expected to talk to me. So I was a good deal surprised to hear it, rich and full, coming to me here through the receiver.

I asked him if he would mind letting me talk over some new aspects of the Marshall case with him, and offered to go to his quarters if he would receive me.

"I am afraid you wouldn't find them very comfortable," he said, "but I'll be glad to come to see you."

Upon that understanding, I ordered up a siphon and some ice, and got out a square bottle and some cigars. He lived not far away, and it was less than ten minutes before I heard his ring. I felt a certain return of confidence, quietness, and poise come to me just with the sight of him.

His voice lasted through the first few words of his greeting and then apparently left him for good. I soon got used to the whisper, however, and forgot it.

I put him into my easiest chair and told him, under the stimulus of his grave, keen attention, and a whispered question here and there, the whole story, so far as I knew it, of the last twenty-four hours and of the events that had led up to it.

"I am rather interested," he observed at last, "in what you tell me of the other man—the doctor whom Mrs. Marshall says her husband ruined years ago. Tell me all you can about him. In the first place, did she say quite definitely that he was dead?"

"No," said I thoughtfully, "she spoke as if he was dead, spoke of it rather bitterly and with a good deal of personal feeling. It was not through her husband that she knew about it. It seems that he—James Hyde, his name was—was a sort of cousin of her own, a good deal older, but not too old for a romantic young girl to take an interest in. He was an extremely handsome man, she says, with a great charm of manner. From her description, he had a most brilliant mind, which he could turn to anything, although he had a special genius for medicine. He was guilty, it seems, of little worse than an indiscretion—talking about some patient of his, I believe, in a way that was unprofessional, perhaps, but not malicious—and Dr. Marshall simply hounded him out of the city; 'pushed him down off the curve of the world,' was the way she put it. And now I remember what she said about his death. She said she 'did not know in what miserable slough of despair he might have perished.'

"Evidently the incident made a lasting impression on her mind, for she had taunted her husband with it on the very morning of his death, and she talked about it at considerable length to me this evening. But her belief in Hyde's death is evidently based on pure assumption."

Our conversation got diverted just then, owing to a little accident. A careless motion of his arm knocked the siphon off the little tabouret that stood beside his chair, and broke it, and the moment of mild excitement which this provided us with had the curious effect of restoring his voice.

It was he who commented on the fact. "It always acts that way," he said. "I can speak perfectly well through the telephone if the conversation doesn't last too long. The affection is purely nervous. It has nothing to do with the organs of the throat themselves. It is my firm belief that if I could get the chance, I should be able to play my parts on the stage just as well as ever, but of course it is absurd to expect any manager to risk it."

"But does an actor's excitement last after the first minute or two?" I asked.

"Excitement is hardly the word for it. There is an increase in the nervous tension. I think the mere effort involved in keeping myself in another character than my own would prevent my voice from failing me."

"Isn't there a chance of your getting some manager to risk it?"

He shook his head. "Not the least in the world. I must find some other way of making a living; some way that the possession of a voice is not essential to. Then, perhaps, when I don't want it, it will come back again. But that's enough about me. Let's go back to our mystery."

"Do you think," I asked, "that there may be something in the theory that this doctor whom he ruined has come back after all these years and avenged himself upon him?"

Of course I was merely echoing the thought that I knew was in Mr. Stancliffe's mind, but I wanted him to develop the idea more thoroughly. It made it seem rather promising.

"I don't know," he said very thoughtfully, after a little silence. "They testified, if the newspaper reports of the inquest are correct, that the murder had, in all probability, been committed by a doctor; the coroner's physician, in fact, spoke of it as a 'surgical operation' rather than a murder. But the other theory, especially in view of what young Marshall told you, the woman theory, seems better. Unless Dr. Marshall was deliberately submitting to an examination by a doctor, no man could have got around behind his chair and touched his face with his hands. Going farther than that, the very first faint prick of steel, unless it were expected, would have caused an instantaneous resistance.

"But those difficulties quite shortly disappear if you adopt the theory that it was a woman. She might have got behind the doctor's chair, have touched his face with her hands, by way of a caress, and the imperceptible instant during which he might have jerked away would have been lost. He would have accounted for the prick with the thought of a pin in the waistband, perhaps. His whole attitude of mind and body, at least, would have been quite different with a woman behind him, a charming and attractive one, say, than with a man. On the whole, I think that counteracts the presumption established by the apparent knowledge of the location of the jugular vein."

"Do you mean his wife?" I asked.

"No," he said, "I mean the woman we know was in the office with him—the girl who testified she went out at twenty minutes to twelve."

"You mean the last patient!" I cried. "Gwendolen Carr, a slender frail little thing like that?"

"This wasn't a crime of violence. That's the very essence of it. Sandow never could have accomplished it, because his purpose would have been frustrated by the faintest resistance. The very prettiness and innocence and charm, which seem to have made such an impression on you, would be worth more in a crime like that than the strength of twenty men."

"Well," I confessed rather ruefully, "I have suspected nearly everybody, but it never occurred to me to think of her."

"That's because all the testimony had so obvious a direction. When you look at the case without prejudice, there's a good deal of ground for suspicion against her. She is the last person known to have seen him alive, in the first place; and in the second place, there was an obvious lack of candor about her testimony at the inquest."

"It wasn't obvious to me," said I.

"Oh, but you weren't looking. Do you remember when the coroner asked her if her visit to the doctor was of a professional character? This was her answer, 'Do you mean did I go as a patient? Yes, sir.' Of course she went as a patient. She took her place in the line in the reception room and waited her turn. If the doctor had already refused to see her on any other terms, this would afford her an easy means of access to him; the only means, very likely, unless she wanted to make a scene somewhere, and she doesn't seem to be the kind of person to do that."

"It seems to me you are attributing a curious confusion to her character in supposing that she would be willing to murder a man in cold blood, and yet would risk an equivocation instead of a downright lie when questioned about it."

"Women are like that," he said, "and, then, too, God knows the poor thing may have been justified."

I took ten minutes or so to digesting that theory, in silence. It was utterly new to me, utterly repugnant to my instincts to entertain it, and yet, in many ways, it seemed to square remarkably with the facts.

Suddenly, however, I thought of something. "But there's Jack," I cried. "Where does he come in? If he had happened to see her coming out of his father's office at twenty minutes past twelve, instead of twenty minutes before, as she testified, what in the world could keep him from saying so?"

But I saw the answer before Mr. Stancliffe's whispering voice could put it into words. "Suppose Jack knew," he answered; "knew something, no matter what, that involved this girl to his father's discredit. Wouldn't he hold back that knowledge as long as he could?"

His question clearly needed no answer, and I made none, but sat thoughtfully silent, with my chin in my hands, turning over in my mind this new and disquieting angle which the case had taken.

"There are a few minor points that are also worthy of consideration. In the first place, while her speech and manner are those of a person of education and refinement, her dress is not that of a young woman of wealth. It is inconspicuous and shows a considerable regard for economy. You must permit me, as an actor, to speak in such matters as one having authority. She gives her address as the St. Anthony. A person who found it necessary to economize in matters of dress would hardly be living at the newest and most luxurious hotel in New York. She would not be likely to go to consult Dr. Marshall professionally. If she comes from out of town and is only a transient at that hotel, she would have someone with her. She would not have gone alone to the doctor's office.

"I have just this much more to add: remember that I was in Dr. Marshall's waiting room myself that morning. She was only three or four behind me in the line of waiting patients, and I had a good chance to observe her. It occurred to me at the time that I could not ask an actress better to portray a strong, self-contained, well-bred young woman, waiting for the beginning of what must prove a painful scene, than this Miss Gwendolen Carr did while I sat there watching her."

The telephone bell rang just then. It was the call I had been expecting but had forgotten. Madeline herself was on the wire.

"Jack came in about an hour ago," she said. "He must have been having a fearful time. He was mud stained and exhausted, and in a raging fever. He is delirious now. I am afraid he is going to be seriously ill."

When she had rung off, I told Mr. Stancliffe the upshot of our conversation. "So there will be nothing to be got from him for an indefinite time. What do you say to our going up to the St. Anthony and seeing Miss Carr ourselves?"

"We shall be too late to find her," said Mr. Stancliffe, "but we may as well go up there and see what we can find out about her."

"Why do you think we shall be too late?" I asked.

"I suspected it before, but Mrs. Marshall's message made me sure of it. It was undoubtedly this Miss Gwendolen Carr whom Jack went to see; undoubtedly, that is, unless our whole theory of the case is wrong. Well, he couldn't have got into the mud between the St. Anthony and his own house. She's gone away to someone of the suburbs, you may take my word for it."

We put on our hats, however, lighted fresh cigars, and set out for the St. Anthony. It was I who walked up to the clerk to make our inquiry.

"Is Miss Gwendolen Carr stopping here?" I asked.

His face was wooden enough already, but at the sound of that name it turned perfectly expressionless. "Not here," he said.

"Can you tell me when she left?"

"Never been here, I think," he said. "Look at the register, if you like."

I didn't believe him; at least I was sure that the name was familiar to him, and that he could probably have told me more than he did. But I saw nothing better to do than to open the register, and begin to turn over the pages.

After spending a few minutes at this profitless occupation, I felt a touch on my elbow. "Come," said Mr. Stancliffe, "I always begin to feel the need of a shave about this time in the evening. Let's go down to the barber shop."

I had no idea what he was driving at, and he would not tell me. But I was not kept waiting very long. The moment he settled down in the first barber's chair, he gave his head a knowing nod in the direction of the manicurist's table in the corner.

"Got a new one, I see," he said.

"You knew her, did you?" asked the barber, with a look of perfect comprehension.

Mr. Stancliffe nodded indifferently. "What's become of her?" he asked.

"Search me," said the barber. "She got the sack from here when she gave this hotel as her address at the coroner's inquest in the Marshall case. It happened to be true; she did live here, but that excuse didn't go down with the management. She had orders to pack up as soon as they read the evening papers."

"You don't happen to know where she's gone?"

The barber waved his hand. "Somewhere between Hackensack and Staten Island, I should say. I can't do better than that."

X

Mr. Stancliffe's Trap

Somewhere between Hackensack and Staten Island," or, if the barber's mind had worked east and west, instead of north and south, he might as well have said, "Somewhere between Newark and Flushing." Somewhere among the other four million in this congested little corner of the world. It seemed to me, as I and my companion emerged from the hotel and started walking southward down the avenue together, that any attempt to find her would be perfectly hopeless.

I said as much to Mr. Stancliffe. "And yet it is equally clear," I went on, "that she's got to be found. Whether or not she murdered Dr. Marshall, and I still find that difficult to believe, there is no doubt that she knows a great deal more of the matter than she told the coroner. Of course it may be a wild-goose chase altogether; we can't tell about that until Jack Marshall is well enough to talk again, but that won't be for several days, and it may be never. We do know, or practically know, at least, that Dr. Armstrong is innocent, and we can't leave him disgraced and in despair locked up there in the Tombs."

"I am not so sure that it would prove a very difficult matter to find her," said Mr. Stancliffe. "Apparently, Jack Marshall did."

"I suppose it might be done," I assented, "but I haven't the slightest idea how to set about it. My wits seem to be paralyzed somehow in this business. I begin to suspect myself—no, not of being the murderer, but of being a great fool."

"Oh, that doesn't follow," said my companion easily. "The one essential thing to a detective is a sense of complete detachment. A man whose personal sympathies, likes, dislikes, affections are aroused in any case is, in the nature of things, powerless. Sherlock Holmes would have been if somebody had murdered Dr. Watson."

"There may be something in that," I admitted, "yet, I doubt if I am cut out for a detective anyway. I was too ignorant to spot Pomeroy's ruby for an imitation. I was too inattentive to note the suspicious circumstance which you pointed out to me in the case of Miss Carr's testimony. I hadn't any personal interest in either of them. And yet the police are worse than I am. If we were to put this line of evidence into their hands, the first thing that they would do would be to take the whole Metropolitan press into their confidence, and fan the spark into a perfect blaze of scandal inside of twenty-four hours. And by that time Miss Gwendolen Carr would be lost indeed."

"You are quite right," he assented. "There's nothing to be done in that direction."

We walked on for two or three blocks, perhaps, in silence. I was pondering upon an idea of mine, which I didn't quite dare to put into words. But at last he turned to me with a smile. "You're quite right. An actor, without a voice and living in a little boarding house on West Twenty-seventh Street, can fairly be presumed to be somewhere near the end of his financial tether."

I simply stared at him aghast, for the thing he said was the thing that was in my mind, only it had remained unspoken.

"Oh," he went on easily, "it didn't require a C. Auguste Dupin to follow the train of *your* thoughts. You were wishing that I would undertake to find Miss Carr for you, and wondering if you dared offer to pay me."

"Well," said I, making a virtue of a necessity, "if I did think of it, and the thoughts that come to one are not subject wholly to his own volition, I had, at least, the grace to refrain from passing on the suggestion to you. There is no offense, I trust."

"None whatever."

He did not speak again until, at our slow pace, we had covered another block. Then he said, quite abruptly, "I am not without the prospect of a livelihood, at least for a while. One of these new magazines has entered into an arrangement with me to write a series of sketches of some of the character parts I have taken in famous plays. My part of the work is really little more than to provide the letter press for a series of drawings, for which I am to pose as the characters themselves. The artist is no less a person than your friend, Mr. Arthur Jeffrey. But that is for the future, at least the payment is. For the immediate present I am, or was until this evening, almost at a loss which way to turn. If you think my services as a detective are worth anything, I am very glad."

I could not accept his offer without a little protest. "It's not a fit sort of work for me to let you do. It's not the sort of thing a gentleman should be asked to stain his hands with."

"My dear young friend," said he, "it was not because it was disagreeable that you hesitated to undertake it yourself, but because you thought, and quite rightly, that you weren't competent to do it. I believe I am, and I am very glad of the ability to do you a service. As for staining one's hands, a knock-about character like an actor stains his often enough; and, then, one always can wear gloves."

With that mild joke, we let the subject drop and talked of other matters, until we reached the point downtown where our ways divided. Then we came down to business, and had a good-humored little quarrel about terms, he protesting against those I offered as too high. We soon came to an amicable understanding, however.

"Don't worry about it," was his parting injunction. "I shall find her, never fear. When I do, I will let you know."

For the next two days I did what I could to follow his instructions and stop worrying about the Marshall mystery. I made a point of seeing nothing whatever of any person however remotely connected with it. I took pains to avoid even Jeffrey, the regularity of whose daily routine made it an easy matter. The only thing I did was to call up the Marshall house once a day on the 'phone and inquire about Jack. He was still very, very ill, and the two physicians who were in daily attendance on him adopted the reassuring, encouraging tone which all who know anything of desperate illness and waning hopes are alike familiar with.

I contrived to do my own work, which was sadly in arrears, in a certain dull routine fashion, and by means of an extremely active pair of mental pruning shears, managed to nip in the bud the various guesses, theories, and hazards which my mind kept putting forth about the scene of the murder. I would do as I was told, and wait to hear from Mr. Stancliffe.

One night, two or three days after the funeral, when I returned to the apartment after a long day's work, the desk clerk cheered me with the information that a gentleman was waiting to see me, a clean-shaven gentleman who had lost his voice.

"Where is he?" I asked.

"When we told him that you were out, sir, he inquired if Mr. Jeffrey was in, and learning that he was, decided to wait for you there."

In Jeffrey's rooms! Oh, of course it was all natural enough. He and Jeffrey were working together for this magazine series, but I could not help wondering, as I rode up in the elevator, whether, by any possibility, Mr. Stancliffe could have run on some clew that would give him reasonable data for the same suspicion which my own mind so vaguely and irrationally entertained against the young artist.

I simply called a good evening to Jeffrey through the door, and told Mr. Stancliffe I was ready to see him. We had comfortably settled down in my sitting room before we exchanged a word.

"He is an enigma I find it difficult to solve," said I, nodding in the direction of my friend's apartments. "I think I told you of that note from Mrs. Marshall I saw on his table."

"In other words," said he, "you are inclined to suspect him of some connection with our mystery?"

"Oh, I know I haven't the slightest reasonable ground for it," I answered, half apologetically.

He laughed. "You'll do well to take one thing at a time, at any rate," said he. "If our theory about Miss Carr and the doctor proves to be a mare's nest, it will be time enough to look about for another one."

"You are quite right," said I. "Well, how does it go? Have you any hope of finding her?"

"I have found her. Here's her address." He handed me a card as he spoke. "And you'll observe that Jack had an ample excuse for getting in the mud. The address is in Flatbush, or rather in a suburb of it. She's living quite by herself in a boarding house."

From the point of view of a confirmed New Yorker, the place seemed incredibly remote. "And you've actually found her," said I; "not only found her, but found her in a place away off a thousand miles from anywhere. I don't see how you did it."

"It didn't prove difficult. Miss Carr, although she dresses inconspicuously and talks in a soft voice, is not the sort of person who would find it easy to lose herself. She has too much personal color. A person who had enjoyed one good look at her would not only recognize her on seeing her a second time, but would remember that he had seen her, if he only saw her once. Of course the St. Anthony was the starting point. She had been employed there for some time, and it was obvious she could not have been there long without arousing the keen personal interest of a good many people. It was only a question of appearing in the right character and asking the right kind of questions of the right people. The rest proved easy enough. At all events, there she is."

"Have you talked to her? "I asked. "Has she told you anything?"

"I have not even seen her, or, rather, she's not seen me. I am leaving that part of it to you."

"I think you could do it better," I urged. "My powers of penetration seem to be under an eclipse."

"This is my suggestion," said he: "that you go out, find her, tell her quite simply your position in the case, and ask her to come to New York with you. I advise you to tell her frankly that you want to take her up to Dr. Marshall's office; that there are some matters of detail that you wish to satisfy yourself about, and it will be easier to clear them up there on the spot than anywhere else. I think you told me you knew Cromwell, the district attorney. In that case, you will have no trouble in getting permission to look over the premises, which I suppose are still under police guard. As for me, you can pick me up on the way, and we will all go together."

"Do you think she'll come?"

"I'm inclined to think so, yes. There is no reason for making her think that you suspect her of anything. She's come through so far without suspicion. On the other hand, if she refused to come, in spite of your urgent request, that refusal would, of itself, direct suspicion against her. She'll see that, I think, and come like a lamb."

I hated the job heartily. "Come like a lamb," indeed! like a lamb to the slaughter! But there was nothing else for it, so I went. The task was not made easier by the strong conviction, which had been growing upon me as I summed up the case against her, that if not guilty of the actual murder itself, she at least had guilty knowledge of it.

All the length of my long ride in the subway and the elevated I felt a good deal as a jailer must feel when he has to read a death warrant.

I found the house without as much difficulty as I had anticipated. It was in a rather lonely neighborhood, but a comfortable-looking place enough.

When I ascertained that I had come to the right place, and that Miss Gwendolen Carr was at home, or "in," as the domestic, who answered the bell, expressed it, I simply sent in my card, without explanation, and asked if I might see her. I took my seat in the cheerless little parlor which the servant indicated, heard her heavy footsteps ascending the stairs, heard a door open and a low-voiced conversation.

After that, I thought I heard a little half-choked cry. Then came descending footsteps, lighter ones and more hurried, and the next moment Miss Gwendolen Carr stood in the doorway.

I could hardly repress an exclamation of astonishment at the sight of her face. The pallor of it might be the result of a shock, or a premonition received only a moment ago, but the haggard, hunted look it wore was not a matter of moments, but of days. When I first saw her there in

Dr. Marshall's office the evening she identified Pomeroy, I instinctively described her to myself as a girl. Now I should describe her as a woman, a woman wearing an invisible veil of tragedy.

Evidently she had identified me from my card, though how, I was at a loss at first to discover. Afterwards I remembered that she had been sitting in the doctor's reception room that night when Jack and I came in, and that I had given my name to the sergeant. So she manifested no surprise at the sight of me.

But, in fact, the tragic horror in her face was far beyond surprise. Her hands opened and shut convulsively, once or twice, and then she clasped them together in front of her before she spoke. "Have you something to tell me?" she asked. "Have you something dreadful to tell me?" Before I could find words with which to frame a reply she went on:

"Did he—Is he—"

It was simply impossible to look upon an agony like that and make no attempt to alleviate it. I suppose if I were a born detective, I should have played upon her fears, misled her, trapped her in that moment when grief made her defenseless, and pieced together her whole story, whatever it was. There was a story there plainly enough. But, as I say, I could not do it.

"Sit down, Miss Carr," I said. "Please, please don't distress yourself. I've brought no news for you whatever. I came out here to ask you a favor."

With a long sigh, which told me that I had only half succeeded in reassuring her, she seated herself and I followed her example.

"Miss Carr," said I, "there are still a few details connected with Dr. Marshall's death which are very obscure to us. Young Mr. Marshall was taken ill on the day of the inquest and is not yet in condition to take charge of the family affairs, is not even able as yet to tell us what he himself may know. So at present that duty devolves on me. It has occurred to me, and to one of my friends, that if you will go with us to Dr. Marshall's office, you may be able to clear up some things that puzzle us. I said it was a favor I had to ask, and I repeat that that is the way I regard it. We shall be under a very great obligation to you if you will come."

It was some little time before she made me any answer. It did not seem precisely as if she hesitated, but rather as if her mind were following out some line of thought of her own. There was no evidence of alarm about her manner either; indeed, she seemed distinctly more self-possessed than she had been when she first came into the room.

I did not repeat my question, however, but waited in silence, and at last she answered it. "Yes, I'll go with you," she said simply, and rose as if to leave the room in quest of her wraps, but at the doorway she paused a moment.

"I can't pretend that it won't be very painful to me," she said, "more painful than you had any cause to suspect when you came out here, but I realize that it isn't your fault. You had to come and I must go with you."

The ride back to town was rather ghastly; that was my feeling about it, at any rate. Mr. Stancliffe had been too wise to take me very far into his confidence, but I was able to guess that there in Dr. Marshall's office would be found some trap, ready to spring and hold fast, the moment her unwary foot had trodden on it.

It would have been horrible enough to take her there in any case, but she made it worse by her brave attempt to spare me the discomfort of witnessing her own agony. All the way back to town she held her dainty head erect, and though words half choked her, made conversation for me, talked brightly, even wittily, about such indifferent subjects as we could find in common. There was no trace of bravado about it. She was simply trying to spare me an acute discomfort. It was, I think, the finest exhibition of courage I have ever seen.

Before we reached our rendezvous with Stancliffe, I told her about him, and I think I succeeded in diverting her mind a little by my recital. I prepared her for his queer, whispering voice, and told her something of the interest he had been taking in our mystery. "He gives me the feeling, somehow," said I, "that eventually he will solve it."

"I hope he may," she said, in a voice little above a whisper; "oh, how I hope he may!"

Was her little exclamation spontaneous or calculated? I would have given a good deal to know. It sounded spontaneous to me.

We met Mr. Stancliffe in the entrance to the Grosvenor, and on alighting from the elevator and presenting the pass which I had secured, we were at once admitted to the doctor's reception room.

My friend surprised me by seeming to pay very little attention to the girl, certainly subjected her to no close scrutiny while we sat there talking. He recalled to her mind the fact that he had only been three or four ahead of her in the line, and asked her a few questions, irrelevant enough, chiefly about the patients who had intervened between them and had been in to see the doctor after he himself had seen him and gone away.

He also spoke of Pomeroy, and asked rather particularly when he had gone out. His place in the line had been just ahead of Miss Carr's. It was plain enough to me what he was doing. He was putting her at her ease, quieting her suspicions; getting her mind off its guard, so that his trap, when it should be sprung, should catch her utterly unawares.

Finally he rose. "I know it will be painful to you, Miss Carr," he said, "and I dislike to have to ask you to do it, but would you be willing to come with us into the inner office here?"

She turned a little paler, but assented to his request, as a matter of course.

With a word of apology, he went in first. I followed her, and at Mr. Stancliffe's request, closed the door behind us.

"Now," said he cheerfully, "after another detail or two we shall be done. What chair did you sit in during your interview with the doctor, Miss Carr?"

"This one," she answered promptly, indicating it with her hand.

"Whereabout in the room was it?"

"Almost exactly where it is standing now."

"Do you mind sitting down in it?"

"Not at all."

"May I ask you, Mr. Drew, to sit down in Dr. Marshall's chair behind the desk?" Then, turning to her, "It was there that he sat, was it not, during your interview, Miss Carr?"

"Yes," she answered.

"Did he remain in that chair throughout your whole interview?"

"Yes."

"And you in yours?"

She was finding it more and more difficult to answer his questions. Her last "yes" was in almost as soundless a whisper as that in which the question was asked.

"You stayed in that chair, then, until the interview was closed and you got up to leave the room?"

"Yes."

"And then did you walk straight to the door and open it?"

I hardly heard her answer, though I was aware, vaguely, that it was in the affirmative.

For the first time, since I had taken my seat in the swivel chair behind the desk, my eyes left her face. I wonder if the direction they took was the result of an unconscious telepathic suggestion from the powerful mind of the other man in the room. Where I looked was at a point on the wall behind her, five or six feet above her head, where the clock hung.

And then I saw Stancliffe's trap, or thought I did, for he had set the hands of that clock so that they pointed to twenty minutes past twelve.

"You went straight to the door?" Mr. Stancliffe asked. "Show us how you did it."

She sat quite still for a second, to steady herself. Then rose, and, without a backward glance, walked toward the door and laid her hand on the knob.

"You said something in your testimony before the coroner about looking at the clock just as you were opening the door." She stood perfectly still where she was, waiting for him to finish his sentence.

His whispered command, when he went on, had a sort of horrible menace in it: "Look at the clock now, Miss Carr."

To do so, she would have to turn quite around. To my astonishment, that was not what she did at all. She turned, instead, a little, a very little to the right and looked into the great mirror. Then she gasped a little and looked around quickly at Mr. Stancliffe. "That's—that's the time it was when I went out."

"What time?"

"Twenty minutes before twelve; the time I said."

"You are looking at the clock in the mirror, Miss Carr. Turn and look at it on the wall."

She did not do so at once. It seemed for a moment as if she did not understand, and she looked at me instead, as if for further enlightment. But at last she followed the direction of his own look, and glanced at the clock.

One glance was enough. "Twenty minutes *after*!" she whispered. And then from Mr. Stancliffe's face to mine, and from mine back to his, she turned, in an agonized sort of bewilderment and horror.

Then she swayed a little where she stood, and fainted.

XI

Ten Minutes Left

For the next moment or two there was no time to think. We were confronted, as the saying goes, by a condition and not a theory; the temporarily lifeless condition of the pallid young beauty who lay there on the floor at our feet. Beside the imperative necessity of doing something, I was conscious only of a feeling of rather childish irritation that in this emergency, as in so many others, Mr. Stancliffe should prove a more competent man than I. He knew what to do and he did it, while I stood busily around doing nothing, or at least accomplishing nothing.

The moment the fluttering eyelids and the tremulously indrawn breath gave a hint of returning consciousness, my friend turned to me, with a brisk word of command.

"Open the door," said he, "and call in that policeman from the reception room. Then the two of you together carry this couch out into the outer room. We'll put her on it and give her a chance to get her strength and her wits together again before we ask her any further questions."

"Why take her out there?" I asked.

"Because I want to talk things over with you privately, and it would be inhuman to leave her in here alone. Not only inhuman, but possibly dangerous. But out there the policeman can keep an eye on her without seeming to."

When we had left her, comfortably ensconced on the couch under the curious eye of the policeman, who had a hint that it would be as well to keep his eye upon her, we withdrew once more into that horrible inner office.

"How in the world," I asked when the door closed behind us, "did you happen to think of it—the trap, I mean?"

"Why," said he, "I had noticed that mirror myself when I was in here earlier that very morning. When I read in her testimony that she looked at the clock as she was opening the door, I thought it possible that she was merely lying. Then, as I thought further about it, the mirror occurred to me, and I saw that she might think that she was telling the truth and think, also, that she was perfectly safe in doing so, the interval between her going out and the finding of the body being sufficient to allow for the commission of the crime."

"Well," said I regretfully, "you have made your case."

"Oh, by no means," he protested. "That's what the police thought when they found Pomeroy's imitation ruby. That's what the district attorney thought when he heard about Armstrong's hypodermic needle. We haven't our case yet by any means, but the first thing to do is to find out exactly what we have got; not what we are able to guess at, but what we actually know. The first thing is a complete alibi for Armstrong. He was in the instrument shop downstairs at a quarter past twelve, and she didn't leave here until twenty minutes past."

"Unless," I suggested, "the murder was the result of a conspiracy between them; unless the two of them were in here together."

"That won't hold water," said Mr. Stancliffe, after a moment's thought. "If they had been in a conspiracy and both been deliberately lying on the stand, the matter of time would have been their first concern. She might have sworn, as she did, that she had left at twenty minutes to twelve, but she would have *known* better and would certainly have evaded my trap.

"Besides, it seems to me it was, in its essence, a single-handed crime. If both of them had been in the room, neither would have been able to get into a relative position with their victim which would have made that needle thrust possible. No, we have cleared the doctor absolutely."

"I suppose you are right in saying the case isn't complete against her, but, upon my soul, it looks complete enough. She was in here for an hour. We know that her visit was not an ordinary professional one. We know there was some relation between them which has not yet been explained by the Marshalls. She went away unseen and unheard, and ten minutes afterwards Dr. Marshall was found murdered."

"You have stated right there the two things we need to make the case complete. First, what was her personal relation with the Marshalls? Was it one that would supply a possible motive for the murder? A well-bred young woman does not deliberately kill a man until she is urged to by some very strong compulsion. We need a motive, and we haven't got it. That, in the first place. And in the second place, my dear young friend, we must account for that last ten minutes before we can sit back and say our case is altogether complete."

"What could possibly have happened in so short time as that?" I asked.

"Don't you remember," said he, "that both the telephone operator and Dr. Armstrong spoke of the murdered man as having had an appointment at twelve o'clock—an important appointment? Neither of them was asked what that appointment was, it is true, but isn't it likely if they had known what it was, they would have volunteered the information? It is possible, at any rate, that both these witnesses are in the dark as to the nature of that important appointment at twelve o'clock. Both of them assumed that he was going out to keep it, but both of them might be mistaken.

"However, we are distinctly making progress. Dr. Marshall was alive at half past eleven; at half past twelve he was dead. For fifty minutes of the hour that poor young girl out there in the reception room was in here with him. For the remaining ten minutes, dead or alive, he was alone, so far as we know."

Without another word to me he opened the door and stepped out into the reception room. Looking over his shoulder I saw that Miss Carr had left the couch and was sitting in an easy chair near one of the windows.

"We don't want to cause you one moment of unnecessary distress," Mr. Stancliffe was saying to her, and his words, in spite of the harsh whispered quality of his voice, or voicelessness rather, sounded gentle. "However, if you feel able to answer a few more questions, I am sure you can help us, and I think it not unlikely that we can help you. Also, since we cannot dismiss the policeman, I would suggest that we go back into the inner office."

She agreed to that without demur. So back we went, and once more the door was shut behind us.

Somewhat to my surprise, Mr. Stancliffe whispered to me that I had better take charge of the interrogation, and it seemed reasonable enough when I came to think of it. He had questioned her before, had led her into a trap, and he was in her mind nothing but a detective. By comparison with him, at any rate, I would seem like a friend. She would probably find my questions easier to answer frankly and fully than she would his.

"If I ask anything, Miss Carr," I began, "that you don't want to answer, you must say so. This isn't an inquisition at all. We both feel that you can tell us more than you have told anyone yet about your interview with Dr. Marshall. We noticed that you evaded telling the coroner, in so many words, that your consultation with the doctor was a professional one."

"It wasn't professional," she said; "it was quite personal. I went to him as a patient simply because he had already declined to see me on other terms."

"Was your purpose in seeking that interview anything that you can confide to us?"

"Yes, I think I can. I think it will be"—her voice broke there, but she swallowed hard and pressed her lips together, and presently commanded it again—"a relief to tell it to somebody. But don't you know about it already? You have talked with Jack—young Mr. Marshall, I mean. Hasn't he told you?"

"What in the world has he to do with it?" I asked.

At her answer I felt like a man looking into a kaleidoscope, who sees a pattern that had looked very complete and symmetrical, suddenly change, at the mere touch of a finger, into something altogether different, for the significance and connection of every detail of the whole mystery suddenly took on a different aspect.

"I was engaged to marry him," she said.

For an instant my mind stood still. Then it went racing back, in the swiftest review of the mystery as it looked with this new light thrown upon it. One thing at least was plainly accounted for. This was, Jack Marshall's demeanor during the twenty-four hours that followed the discovery of the murder. I remembered his half-hysterical laugh when he had said he wished that suicide was a tenable theory. I remembered his astonishment, which at the time I had thought to be assumed, over my own suspicions of his stepmother. I remembered the perfectly ghastly look in his face when he had waited for me in the corridor after the inquest.

And from it all, one inference was horribly clear, namely, that Jack himself had believed, had gone on believing until merciful delirium had sponged out thought altogether, that this girl, his fiancée, the woman he loved, had murdered his father.

After a little silence, she went on speaking. "It isn't quite true that I was engaged to him. I had refused to be—refused to marry him, unless his father would consent. I cared too much for him to run the risk of wrecking his life and his prospects that way."

"Do you mean," I asked earnestly, "that you think it would injure him—well—in a broad sense—socially—to marry—?"

She completed the sentence for me. "Marry a girl who was working at a manicure table in the barber shop of the St. Anthony Hotel? Yes, I do. Don't you think I was right?"

Well, I supposed she was, although the impulse to say, "Not if that girl happened to be you," was a strong one. I evaded answering.

"Was that your—occupation when Jack Marshall made your acquaintance?"

"Yes," she said; "he came in to have his finger nails attended to, and I did the work for him." She hesitated a moment, and then added: "I shouldn't have chosen that way of earning a living if I had had exactly my choice."

"Do you mind telling us a little more about yourself?" I asked. "It's not mere impertinent curiosity. Oh, I am curious, I admit, but that is not why I asked the question. We are really pretty sadly perplexed, Mr. Stancliffe and I."

"Of course I don't mind telling you," she said. "You are quite right to ask. I spent the first eighteen years of my life in Louisville, Ky., and I was brought up with no idea of ever earning my living at all. I can't remember either of my parents. They both died when I was quite a little thing, and the only relative I had was an uncle. He always seemed to have plenty of money, and he let me have my own way and do what I pleased. When I came to New York to learn to sing it was not with any idea of earning a living. It was partly fun and partly ambition, but the ambition was perfectly real, and for the two years that I studied I made progress enough to keep it alive. I worked hard, but I had a good time, and I spent my allowance, which was liberal, religiously every month.

"And then, one day, when my check should have come it didn't, and the next weekly letter that I expected from my uncle didn't come either. A week after that a letter did come from a lawyer, saying that my uncle was dead and that there were no funds to continue the allowance he had been sending me. I had nothing at all but my clothes and some loose change, so I had to do something right away.

"I suppose I might have got a position in the chorus of one of the light opera companies; but you see, I really wanted to learn to sing, and I didn't want to wear my voice out in one of the musical Broadway shows. And then—well, in other ways that sort of work seemed rather more distasteful than the only other thing I could think of doing.

"I did know how to take care of finger nails. I had done it for fun for the girls at home. I had to decide pretty quickly. There wasn't anything else to do, and there wasn't any time for looking about, so the very day I got the lawyer's letter, I applied for work at the St. Anthony Hotel, and got it."

I had to check a disposition to applaud. The quality I most admire, both in men and women, the quality of courage, shone out so splendidly in this simple little recital. There was no word of lament over her fallen fortunes, no disposition to parade the thing she had done as any special virtue. She told it as if what she had done had been the simplest thing in the world—just what anyone else in her circumstances would have done.

"It must have been frightfully hard for you," I observed.

"Oh, it wasn't easy," she assented. "I had to tell myself every night about the thousands of other girls alone here in New York, who had to do just what I did, who had to earn their living, and whose fate didn't matter to any single soul in all the city besides themselves. I had to brace myself up for every day, and every day, at first, I found that I just about lasted until it was over."

"How long had you been at it," I asked, "when you met Jack?"

"It was just a year ago, day before yesterday," she said, "that he came down there into the barber shop for the first time and sat down at the other side of my little glass table."

Her words, unexpectedly to herself it seemed, touched some chord of memory, whose vibrations destroyed for a moment the even self-control with which up to now she had told her story. Her eyes filled suddenly with tears, and her voice faltered. She sat quite still for a moment, holding fast to the arms of her chair and pressing her trembling lips together, letting her tears run as they would down her cheeks. Finally she dried her eyes and sat a little straighter in her chair.

"It was about two weeks ago," she said, "when I told him I would marry him if he could get his father to consent to it. He was to tell his father that we would not marry without his consent. He didn't much want to do it that way. His plan was that we should be married and get his father's forgiveness afterwards, for he was afraid, though he would not admit it at the time, that things would fall out exactly as they did.

"So at last he told his father about it, and told him quite frankly who I was and what I was—how I was earning my living, I mean.

"Dr. Marshall not only refused his consent to Jack's marriage, but he declined absolutely to see me. Jack believed"—she faltered a little over the words—"believed that if he could only see me and talk with me, it would—make a difference. It was his suggestion—Jack's, I mean—that I should go to Dr. Marshall as a patient and then tell him who I was and—and all about myself. I could do that. There was—there is nothing that I am ashamed to tell anybody."

"So you carried out your plan," I prompted her, "came in and told Dr. Marshall who you were. What happened then?"

She shuddered and covered her face with her hands. It will be easy to imagine the feelings with which we waited for her to go on.

Finally I prompted her again. "The interview didn't go as you and Jack had hoped it would. We can see that, and we can imagine that it is painful to you to talk about it. But if you can tell us, I wish you would."

She looked up, straight into my face. Her cheeks were faintly flushed, as if with anger, and her eyes were shining. "I can't tell you what he said. It was unrepeatable, unspeakable. I can't make you understand the utter brutality of it. He took it for granted, the moment he knew who I was, that all I wanted was money—that I was simply a blackmailer. Oh, I can't tell you the words he used—the things he really did say.

"I wanted to go away, but he wouldn't let me; ordered me back into my chair and told me to listen. And then it went on, and on, until I was too sick with disgust to try to answer him, or to go, or to do anything but to sit there with my hands over my ears.

"I didn't kill Dr. Marshall, but I was angry enough to. If he had talked that way to a man, that man would have strangled him as he sat there. When I got up to go I wished I was dead. I didn't want to marry Jack. I felt that I never wanted to see him again, that I never should be able to forget whose son he was.

"But all the time he was waiting for me at the foot of the elevators, waiting with high hopes, I knew, and I had to go down and face him and tell him. He took me somewhere to lunch—I don't remember where—and I tried not to say a word until I was cool again, but thinking about it and trying to talk about it brought all my anger back, as it brings it now.

"And then, what was worst of all, I could see that Jack didn't believe me. He was trying to, but he couldn't—couldn't believe that his father could have done such a thing. So we parted very unhappily—I think he was as utterly miserable as I was—and I went back to work at the St. Anthony Hotel.

"I didn't know Dr. Marshall was dead until I heard them talking about it—the men who were reading the evening papers in the barber shop. And when I heard he was dead I was glad. I was almost glad when I heard that the thief Pomeroy had murdered him. I felt that he deserved it.

"I think you know the rest. I left the St. Anthony the evening after the inquest. I was discharged. Jack came up there just after I had gone, and followed me out to Flatbush, where the woman lives who has, as best she could, been a mother to me ever since I came up to New York with a lot of ambitious notions of becoming a great singer. I shall never forget Jack's face as it looked when I saw him that night. And I found out then—he told me, he had to tell me—that he believed I had murdered his father. He could hardly have helped thinking that. I can understand it now, because he was waiting for me and he knew what time it really was when I came down in the elevator; and he thought—he had to think—that I had lied in my testimony at the inquest. He begged me that night to tell him the truth.

"I heard nothing more from him at all. When you sent up your card to me tonight, I remembered that you were the man who had come up with him to his father's office that night we identified Pomeroy, and I thought that you had come to tell me that he was dead, too. That's what I meant by asking if you had any news for me."

She leaned back in her chair with a little air of relaxation, and drew a long breath or two to steady herself.

"I can't thank you enough," she said, "for bringing me down here and clearing up that mystery about the clock. I am so glad you thought of that. It never would have occurred to me."

"Mr. Stancliffe deserves the credit for it," said I. He was standing at the window staring out, for the recital must have moved him greatly, as it had me. His gloved hands were clasped over the head of his stick, and he was leaning back upon it. He did not look around nor make any answer; just stood there, gazing out over the housetops.

"I have something to hope for now," the girl concluded. "I hope Jack may not die without knowing that I told the truth."

The thought that had come so persistently that first night of the murder came back to me: if only we could find someone endowed with the power which Jeffrey had claimed for himself, the power of reaching the truth, not by the devious ways of evidence, but by the straight short cut of inspiration, for the logic of fact and circumstance had led us into a hopeless bog and left us there.

Not a half hour ago Mr. Stancliffe had said that one of the two things which we needed was a motive. Well, we had it. The girl had confessed to it. Her interview with the doctor had been personal, had led into a violent quarrel—on his part, at any rate. The girl had said in so many words that she was glad when she heard that he was dead; glad, almost, when she learned that he had been murdered. She had left him and gone away from that scene only ten minutes before he had been found dead.

Her story would admit of no halfway acceptance. If the crime had been one of violence in the ordinarily accepted sense, if the doctor had been stabbed with a knife which happened to be lying on the desk, or even shot with a revolver, it might be possible to credit a considerable part of her story and still believe she had committed the crime. It would be conceivable that a brutally insulting attack such as the doctor had made upon her, had brought on an emotional convulsion, during which she had killed him, without premeditation, and almost without consciousness of what she was doing.

But the means that had been taken to accomplish the doctor's murder showed an almost fiendish amount of foresight which could be reconciled with no single word of the girl's story. No, she was either lying from the first word to the last, lying with every look in her eyes and every gesture of her hands, or else she was telling the simple truth. Yet either one of these alternatives led, it seemed, to an impossible conclusion.

Well, we had still the ten minutes left. Would that suffice, a mere six hundred seconds, to bridge the gap between the point where our belief in her story left us and the staring face of the dead thing which the telephone girl saw sitting in what had been his office chair?

It was like Mr. Stancliffe that he wasted no time in such unprofitable speculations. That ten minutes was there, and he went to work upon it at once.

"When you came out of the office into the corridor, Miss Carr, are you sure that you drew the door to behind you? As I remember your testimony, you said Dr. Marshall did not leave his desk."

"I am sure I locked it," she said. "I pulled on the knob until I heard it click, and then pushed back to make sure."

"You met no one, spoke to no one, while you were waiting for the elevator?"

"No, sir."

His next question surprised me. "Were you ever hypnotized?"

"Never, that I know of," she answered.

"Then you never were," he said decisively. "This talk of people being hypnotized for the first time unconsciously or against their will is rubbish."

He took a turn up and down the room. "Well," said he at last, "I think of nothing else to ask you."

She rose and walked swiftly toward the door into the reception room, opened it, and went out, without closing it behind her.

Mr. Stancliffe and I exchanged an inquiring glance. In the face of all the suspicious circumstances which existed against her, had we any right to let her go out to Flatbush, or to take her out there and leave her until we had provided some means of keeping her under surveillance?

"I don't know," I whispered, answering his unspoken question; "I don't know what to believe or where to turn. Do as you think best about it."

He nodded, and then, without telling me his decision, went out into the reception room where the girl was waiting for us.

"I am afraid I rather ran away," she said. "That room will always be a chamber of horrors to me, I fear."

She was pinning on her hat, which we had removed, clumsily enough, when she fainted, and she paused long enough to find the right hole for the hat pin. "It isn't the sight of it that bothers me so much. It's that odor of tobacco. Somehow that brings it all back."

She had been speaking to me. Now she turned to Mr. Stancliffe. "Are you going to let me go home," she asked, "just leaving my word with you that I'll come whenever and wherever you want me, or would you feel better about it if you—?" She did not finish the sentence, but a glance at the half-dormant policeman, supposed to be on watch, completed her meaning.

"No," he said, "your word is all we want."

I nodded, with a feeling of relief. "Then," said I cheerfully, "we'd better be starting on. It's getting late."

"Oh, I shan't allow anyone to go with me," she protested. "That's too horribly far away from town to take a New Yorker."

"As you like," said I. "I'll put you on your car, anyway."

"In that case," said Mr. Stancliffe, "I'll say good night to both of you and remain here for a little. There are a few more matters I want to look into, and now is a good opportunity."

"Shall I come back?" I inquired.

"No," said he; "if I come upon anything of importance I'll telephone you. It is too late to get Armstrong out of the Tombs tonight, but that can be the first thing on our programme tomorrow morning."

As we were going out into the corridor, she paused once more, and turned back to include Mr. Stancliffe in what she had to say. "I can't tell how I thank you. It's been such a relief to tell it all, and especially to get that maddening misunderstanding about the time cleared up. I am going to sleep tonight, all by myself, without the help of a bromide. I haven't done that since—" She finished the sentence with a little gesture.

"I hope so indeed," Mr. Stancliffe said. Then he added: "You are quite sure you don't mind going alone?"

"Not a bit. What's more, I shan't go by the Subway; it's much too fine a night. If anyone went with me, I should feel that I had to take the quickest way."

I hadn't the faintest intention of letting her go out to Flatbush alone, but I said nothing. It would be much easier to waive argument and simply clamber onto the car when it came along.

XII

An Impossible Certainty

My ride back to Flatbush with Gwendolen brought out nothing new in the way of evidence, nothing that a judge or a jury would weigh at a feather's weight in the balances that were to determine this young girl's innocence or guilt. But it decided me at any rate. It was impossible to hear her amplifying her story, giving me an account of the early stages of her acquaintance with Jack Marshall, or to see her hanging on my words when I gave her the full account of the progress of his illness, which had been denied her—impossible to do all this and not reject as utterly grotesque and fantastic the idea that she was a cold-blooded murderess.

I found it easy to understand how the youngster had fallen in love with her. I might have done it myself if it had not been for Madeline. One might get over being in love with Madeline—I had told myself so enough times during the past two years to come to believe it—and still be aware of the utter impossibility of falling in love with anyone else. But I sympathized heartily with poor Jack. Even amidst the surroundings where he had first found her, even in the barber shop at the St. Anthony at her little glass table in the corner, with the implements of her trade spread out before her, her blood and breeding, which even more than her beauty constituted her birthright, must have been instantly evident. The pathos of her incongruity to her garish surroundings would have turned a cooler head than that of a generous, sensitive youngster like Jack Marshall.

The one thing that continued to trouble me as we neared our journey's end was, how had it happened that these obvious facts of Gwendolen's fineness and true gentility had not been apparent to Jack's father? His perceptions were as keen as his son's. His power of disregarding adventitious and superficial appearances and striking straight to the roots was far greater than his son's.

Now that I think back to that time, I am aware that when my mind got to approaching this line of thought, there was one aspect of the case which it refused to look at. Gwendolen herself had spoken of Jack's incredulity on hearing her account of the interview between herself and his father. He couldn't believe, she said, that his father could have said such things, could have treated her with such perfectly wanton brutality. Well, I couldn't believe it either. I had not known Dr. Marshall very well, but the little I had known of him contradicted, in no uncertain terms, her report of his behavior on this occasion. As I say, I refused to look this difficulty in the face. She was so frank, so friendly, so charming, that I turned away like a coward from this troublesome aspect of the case.

We had left the car which had carried us on the last stage of our long journey, and were walking down an ill-lighted and sparsely settled street. The houses were few and were one and all shrouded in darkness. The vacant lots, the broad unbroken zones of deep black shadow, were many.

She was walking with her hand on my arm. "I am disposed to be indignant with you," said I, "for even suggesting that we let you come out here alone at this time of night. You weren't quite truthful then, at any rate, when you assured us you wouldn't be afraid."

"No, that was true," she insisted, "or at least I thought it was then; after the terrors I've been going through these last few days, afraid that Jack would die, afraid that if he lived I should never be able to convince him that I had spoken the truth, even if he ever gave me the chance—after all that, one isn't likely to remember to be afraid in the dark." Then she shivered a little. "But it is fearsome," she said, "and I am not brave naturally. I think I am getting natural again. It's you who have done it, Mr. Drew, you and Mr. Stancliffe. Somehow, since I've told you everything, though it's still terrible and mysterious enough, yet the old nameless horror has left me. I feel like a real person, not like a person in a nightmare. I shall go to sleep tonight without taking any of the stuff the doctor made me take. And, oh, I can't tell you how I thank you."

"It will all come right," said I reassuringly. "I am sure it will."

We were passing just then through a densely shaded patch in the middle of a long block, but ahead of us, two hundred feet perhaps, was a stretch that was better lighted. An opening in the trees allowed the direct rays of an arc light to shine white on the street. Coming toward us through that light we saw a man. He was in the act of vanishing into the same shadow which enveloped us when I glanced up at him, so that I did not see his face.

It did not occur to me that there had been anything alarming about it, until I felt the clutch of Gwendolen's hand on my sleeve. It was sudden, convulsive, involuntary. I was on the outside and would be interposed between him, who ever he was, and the girl, and I felt no alarm for either of us.

I kept on talking in just the same tone I had used before. I don't remember what I said.

The approaching footsteps came nearer. They seemed to hesitate ever so little, and then came on again. The man passed close enough to brush my sleeve, but offered no molestation whatever. The next moment his footsteps were receding behind us.

I expected her, the moment her alarm proved groundless, to laugh a little over her own fears, but to my surprise she did nothing of the sort. I looked at her, when we got out into the light again, and she was certainly very pale.

"Isn't that the house where you live," I asked, "just the other side of this big vacant lot, the first one?"

She did not answer my question. Her voice when she spoke was a mere whisper. "He's stopped," she said. "Do you hear?"

I listened, and was a little surprised not to hear the receding footsteps. "He's probably got out of earshot," said I, "that's all. He must be a good way off by this time."

"No," she said, "it's a still night. We could have heard him for ever so long." Then she looked up at me. "Don't you know who it was?" she asked.

"No, I didn't see his face at all."

"It was Pomeroy," she said. "Don't you remember? The thief who they thought at first must be Dr. Marshall's murderer? It was Pomeroy, I am sure."

I pointed out to her that even if she were right about it, she had nothing to fear from him. My words hadn't much weight, I am afraid. She had been badly frightened, and seemed very anxious about the prospect of my returning to New York alone.

"But I have nothing to fear from him either. He would never in the world try to pick the pocket of a man who might, in all probability, be expected to identify him, and he has no possible motive for attempting anything more serious."

I left her, however, only half reassured.

On my way back to the lonely corner where I must wait for a late car, I kept a sharp lookout for the man we had passed in the dark. I was not at all sure that I might not be attacked, but this was only because I doubted her identification of the man Pomeroy. If it were indeed he, I was safe enough. But I saw nothing of him or anybody else.

I was spared the long wait on the corner I had expected by the timely arrival of a car. For the first time since the Marshall mystery had enveloped me in its folds, I found myself actually feeling sleepy.

The earliest mail next morning brought me a note from Mr. Stancliffe.

> "Don't expect to see anything of me for the next two or three days," he said. "I have got on the track of something that I think may prove important. I haven't time to tell you what it is, and as the situation is one in which you would not be able to assist me, I am going to ask you to do nothing but wait until I have either run it down to the end, or have found that it simply leads back into the fog bank again.
>
> "I am afraid we shall have to leave Dr. Armstrong in jail for a few days longer. We could only secure his release by giving the district attorney all the information we possess about Miss Carr. He would almost certainly have her arrested, or else subjected to surveillance, and either of these courses would be disastrous to my plans. She must remain perfectly free and, so far as she knows, unwatched. Don't communicate with her, and if she writes to you or comes to see you, let me know."

The letter disappointed me a good deal. Evidently enough Mr. Stancliffe was a long way from sharing my belief in Gwendolen's innocence. It was natural, perhaps, that this should be so. He had not gone home with her last night, had not heard her frank and unguarded talk about the whole dreadful business. His impression of her was limited to the comparatively short time when she had been in Dr. Marshall's office and she had been under the restraining influence of the inquisition to which we had subjected her. I wished he had come to me instead of writing, for I felt sure that after a talk with me he would have seen things rather differently.

As the matter stood, however, there was nothing to do but obey his injunction. After all, if she were innocent, as I firmly believed, his clew would, as he put it, only lead back into the "fog bank again."

There were two things, however, which he had left me at liberty to do. One thing was to go to Madeline and tell her that Dr. Armstrong was cleared. Tell her as much as might prove necessary to convince her of this fact, and also to clear myself of the imputation of suspecting that she had had anything to do, directly or indirectly, with her husband's death. The other thing was to go to work myself upon that last ten minutes which still remained unaccounted for.

I did what would, in my own conscience, pass muster for a day's work, and then about five o'clock went up to see Madeline.

She is in many ways—in all sorts of ways, in fact—a wonderful woman. I found her at her tea table, and it seemed as if she read my whole errand instantly in my face, for she came up impulsively and, in that old well-known way of hers, held out both hands to me.

"So you've come back," she said. "I knew you would some day. But you've no idea how good it seems to see you sitting there looking at me without that wild troubled surmise in your face. Tell me all about it."

I couldn't quite do that, but I told her all I could. "We are as far from the end as ever," I concluded, "but the thing is in good hands now and it is going to be solved, I am sure of that." Then I added: "I can't tell how much brighter the world looks now that I know Dr. Armstrong had nothing to do with it."

"I was sure he hadn't. He has done some foolish things. He is awfully serious. He had chanced to see something that happened between Dr. Marshall and me, and he had lost his head about it. I had always liked him and had never pretended that I didn't. He seemed so old and—like a schoolmaster, that I never thought there could be any—danger. But he's very honest and a little quixotic, and if he did do a foolish thing he didn't deserve any such punishment as Dr. Marshall intended for him. It would have been a cruel injustice."

I understood the story, or enough of it, from her fragmentary account. There was no denying her complete candor so far, yet there was one thing left that troubled me a little.

I looked up and found her watching me intently. "Out with it," she commanded. "There is something else."

"I haven't any right to be jealous," I began, "and there is no reason why you should tell me anything that you prefer to keep to yourself—"

"Never mind rights and reasons; what is it?"

"Why," said I, rather lamely, "you and Jeffrey."

"Has he told you anything about that? I especially asked him not to."

"He has told me nothing. I am almost ashamed to confess how slight a thing it is that has troubled me, but, in fact, it was his very silence and yours that did it. I saw a note from you on his table—in your handwriting, that is."

A quick little frown of irritation contracted her brows. I supposed the cause of it was the revelation I had made of my own jealous suspicions, but I soon found I was mistaken.

"That was a perverse little bit of bad luck," she observed. "Of course it troubled you; it would have. And the only reason for the note was to prevent your being troubled. I can't explain it all just now. But Mr. Jeffrey had seen his way to do me—me and Jack—a great service. The note I wrote him was simply to tell him that you had best not be troubled with the matter. I'll explain it all some time. I can't just now. But there's nothing between Mr. Jeffrey and me beyond that, except, of course, that he's awfully interesting and—well, he's a good friend of yours. That counts for him rather heavily in my estimation."

She told me then that the doctors had pronounced Jack to be out of danger. After that we settled down to a good old-fashioned visit.

Altogether, in spite of my disquiet about Gwendolen Carr, I left Madeline's house and started downtown with a feeling of elation such as I had not experienced before in a long, long time. Everything was coming out right. Jack was going to get well. We were going to clear Gwendolen and make the two young lovers happy again. While, as for Madeline—well, I would not play with that idea yet. There was work to be done first. There were those mysterious ten minutes which must be made to give up their tale.

I do not, however, enjoy the advantage of being a man of indefinite leisure. For the next two days a press of work which would admit of no delay prevented me from giving a moment or a thought to the inquiry I was so anxious to begin. But on the third day I determined to leave my office to take care of itself, and start out upon my tour of investigation.

The day began auspiciously with a note handed to me, while I sat at breakfast, from Stancliffe. It was forty-eight hours since I had had any communication from him:

> "Dear Mr. Drew," it read, "I am afraid that in the two days that have elapsed since you have heard from me, you have been thinking of me as either unnecessarily dilatory, or unnecessarily secretive; possibly both. But I really have been very busy and would not have left you in the dark if I could have helped it.
>
> "I really think I am making progress, although when one is working in a labyrinth such as this case of ours has proved to be, one sometimes finds what he thought was progress to be merely a devious and exhausting return to the very point from which he started.

"In one way, I have come back to the starting point. My first intrusion into this case, you will remember, occurred on that night when we walked downtown from the Grosvenor together, and I assured you that Pat Pomeroy's ruby was an imitation and that he was undoubtedly innocent of the murder of Dr. Marshall. If I were asked to go on the stand now and swear to Pomeroy's innocence I should feel a good deal more doubt about it. It is true that his stone was an imitation, and that if he had any complicity in the murder of Dr. Marshall, of which I am by no means sure, the motive was not robbery.

"I have seen the man, however, and am arranging my lines to get an interview with him, not, of course, in my proper person, but in a character under which I hope to gain his confidence. I may say, by the way, that I have never taken so many character parts in forty-eight hours before as I have played since last you saw me in the Grosvenor. I have seen you since, though you do not know where.

"I hope within the next twenty-four hours that matters will develop to a point where I really will have something to tell you.

Faithfully yours,
CARLETON STANCLIFFE

I laid the letter down with a feeling of the liveliest curiosity. Matters must have been progressing rapidly beyond my knowledge if the circle of events had swung clear around again and enveloped Pomeroy. I was half inclined to give over my own projected investigation with the feeling that I was too far behind the present situation to contribute anything to Stancliffe's labors. But a phrase of his own caused me to go back to my original intention. Perhaps, after all, the progress he was making was just a laborious return to the starting point. After all, the thing I had to do was quite clear.

On the presumption of Gwendolen Carr's innocence, the only presumption which my reason found it possible to entertain, the heart of our mystery was contained in the ten minutes between the time when she had left Dr. Marshall alive and Miss Jerome, the telephone operator, had found him dead. If Stancliffe were right in this new suspicion of Pomeroy, my work upon those ten minutes would lead to him just as directly as Mr. Stancliffe's labors would; and I did not see that there could be any possible harm in my trying.

I began the day with a visit to the Grosvenor building. I spent there what was perhaps the most utterly futile hour of my whole career, talking with office boys, elevator men, scrubwomen, and janitors, in the hope of finding someone who could remember the noon hour of that fatal day vividly enough to provide me with a possible clew. I did succeed in getting descriptions of myself, of Stancliffe, and of Gwendolen Carr, and even of Pomeroy, but these descriptions were all evidently *ex post facto* and perfectly useless. I got no facts from any of them that had not already been thrashed out thoroughly in the columns of the daily press.

But it took me about an hour to become convinced of the futility of trying to get anything from them that would serve as a logical clew. Then I turned to what seemed a more promising line of inquiry, and hunted up the telephone girl. When I found her, she was busy and hadn't much time to talk to me. However, in this case my business admitted dispatch.

"It's only one question I want to ask," said I, after she had assured me that she was likely to lose her new job if she spent any time "gassing"—that was her word—with me.

"Only one question. Do you know who it was that Dr. Marshall had his appointment with at twelve o'clock on the day of his murder?"

"Yes," she said shortly. "He had to appear before the commission in lunacy in the Hart case."

Well, that was a blow. I went out of the downtown office where she was employed, feeling all at sea again. Whoever had got into the doctor's office during those ten minutes had been an unexpected visitor.

Not knowing exactly what to do next, I turned north and began strolling slowly up Broadway, hoping that the possible sights and sounds about me would afford some suggestions as to what line of action I should pursue next.

Nothing whatever occurred to me until just as I was passing the New York Life building, with the intersection of Leonard Street just before me. The neighborhood brought back strongly to my mind the day of the inquest, and the sight of the Tombs, only a block away to the right, gave me the idea of going to see Dr. Armstrong.

In fact, my conscience smote me suddenly for having deferred the visit so long. He, rather than Madeline, was entitled to the first tidings that he was cleared from the dreadful appearance of guilt which must almost have overwhelmed him. We could not get him out of jail until

Stancliffe's researches had gone far enough to enable us to put the real criminal, or at least one more strongly under suspicion, in his place. But he, at least, might have the cheering news that the substitution would soon be made.

The formality of getting permission to visit him was easy of accomplishment to a man in my profession, and so it happened that just before the end of visiting hours I found myself in a corridor looking through an iron grating at the pale, troubled face of the man I had last seen on the witness stand at the inquest.

Evidently he read the good news in my face. The sudden brightening of his eyes at the sight of me moved me much more than I had expected the visit to do. I had never seen Armstrong except for the hour he was on the stand, and the one thing I knew about him outside of what he revealed there—namely, that he had been the means of precipitating a quarrel between Madeline and her husband, and of putting her for a while in a distressingly false light in the eyes of her friends—that one piece of knowledge had not tended to make me like him.

But his sufferings were written plainly on his face, and the sight of them and the knowledge that they had been brought upon him by no more serious faults than an absence of humor and a quixotic temperament, caused me to extend my hand to him through the bars, with a feeling of genuine cordiality which surprised myself no less than it did him.

"Dr. Armstrong," said I, "my name is Drew. You may have heard Mrs. Marshall speak of me. I have come to tell you that you are cleared."

"Do you mean it?" he asked, in a voice that was hardly articulate. "Do you mean really clear, or only that you have found a reasonable doubt in my favor?"

"No, I mean just what I said. You are clear," I repeated. "When the world knows what I know now, it will think of you only as an absolutely innocent man who has been most cruelly wronged by circumstances. No sane man will be able to hold any other opinion."

He dropped my hand, clenched his own together and extended them above his head.

"Thank God!" he said, and the words were more a prayer than an exclamation. "Thank God! I hardly believed this day would ever come."

"I am sorry," said I, "that we are not at liberty to go at once to the district attorney with our information and get you out of here. We have not been able to take the police into our confidence, and until we have gone a step or two farther it is critically important that certain persons should not be alarmed, as they would be by your release."

"Don't think of me," he protested eagerly. "Leave me here as long as you like. I shall be glad of the quiet and seclusion which even this dreadful place can afford to a man with a quiet mind." Then he turned to me with a rather curious expression in his eyes.

"I take it from what you say," said he, "that you as good as have your hand upon the murderer. You could hardly so completely clear me without that."

"We don't know as much as we could wish to know," said I cautiously.

"I confess," said he, "I almost find it in my heart to hope he may escape. The man he killed was a—no, he was not a devil—and that is what I started to say. He was only a singularly perfect machine; as brilliant, as perfect, as infallible as the finest machine, and as completely without heart or mercy. If you fell in his way he ground you up. I had so fallen, and all that saved me was the act of someone who may have been his victim, even as I was. I should not have killed him. I was more likely to have destroyed myself; but I will tell you this—that my heart raised a song of savage joy when I found him dead."

His words were startling enough in themselves, but they were doubly so to me, because they echoed the thought of Gwendolen Carr. I remembered how she had said, while affirming her innocence of the crime she saw we imputed to her: "When I read in the papers that he was murdered I was glad; I felt that he deserved it."

"Of course," said I, "no man has the right to absolve the guilty from punishment for their crimes, and even if one were disposed to do so the punishment of the guilty is often the only way of clearing the innocent. Indeed, in this case the person whose testimony clears you, the person who was in Dr. Marshall's office from some time after eleven until twenty minutes past twelve, that person I firmly believe to be innocent; but that person cannot possibly be cleared until the true criminal is discovered."

He looked at me in a curious way.

"You say you know that a certain person was in Dr. Marshall's office continuously from a little after eleven until twenty minutes past twelve. The doctor was alive at the earlier hour; he was dead at the later."

"No," said I. "It was ten minutes after that person had gone out when Miss Jerome went into the office and found the doctor dead. We have still that ten minutes to account for."

He drew his breath sharply, as if about to speak, then checked himself, and for a moment turned abruptly away from the grating. He seemed to be keeping back something, something of importance that he might have said. I waited in silence for him to speak.

"Do you mind if I make a suggestion?" he said at last. "Go up to the Grosvenor and see Dr. Adams. He did something that I did not do. He made a fairly careful examination of Dr. Marshall's body when he was called down at twenty-five minutes to one. He may be able to be of service to you."

A bell rang then which announced the termination of the visitors' hour. Again I extended my hand through the grating.

"Good-by," said I. "I hope I may renew our acquaintance under more auspicious circumstances."

"Good-by," said he, but he seemed loath to let me go. "One question more," he asked. "Does—does Mrs. Marshall know the facts you have told me?"

"Yes," said I, "I told her first of all."

I left the jail with the feeling that at last I had really accomplished something, slight though it might be. Dr. Armstrong's suggestion that I go and see Dr. Adams was clearly a good one. I ought to have thought of it myself. I expected, indeed, nothing positive from him, but it was clear that his negative testimony in a certain direction might prove valuable.

I went straight uptown to the Grosvenor, but was too late to find him at his office there. He had gone home. So I inquired his house address, and followed him thither. Here, at last, I was successful. He was at home and would see me.

He proved to be a large, gray man, with an aquiline nose and an authoritative manner. He didn't seem especially pleased to see me, particularly not after I had told him the nature of my errand. But he waited rather grudgingly to hear what I had to ask of him.

"It has occurred to me," said I, "that you might be able, from the condition of Dr. Marshall's body when you examined it, to fix the hour of his death—"

"Not with any degree of accuracy," the doctor answered; "not at all."

"You couldn't feel at all sure, then," I asked, "that he had been killed within, say, ten minutes of the time you saw the body?"

He stared at me. "*Ten minutes*?" he repeated. "What are you talking about? I am perfectly willing to swear that he had *not* been killed within ten minutes, if that is what you want. When I saw the body at twenty-five minutes to one, he had been dead at least an hour."

"There certainly must be some doubt—" I began.

"Not a doubt in the world," he answered shortly. "No possible doubt, except in the mind of an ignorant fool. Go down to the Tombs and ask Armstrong, if you don't care how much time and how much shoe leather you waste. Ten minutes, indeed!"

There was no need of asking Dr. Armstrong. I knew already what his answer would be. No, the last gate of escape had closed. Gwendolen had gone into Dr. Marshall's office some time before half past eleven. The doctor was alive then. And at twenty-five minutes to one he had been dead for an hour. Gwendolen had not left the office until twenty minutes past twelve.

Admitting these facts to be true—and the only one susceptible of doubt was the correctness of the doctor's opinion—admitting them to be true, they amounted to a mathematical demonstration that the young girl had either murdered the doctor herself, or had seen him murdered before her eyes. In either case, the story she had told to Stancliffe and me was a lie from beginning to end.

I was walking along a quiet cross street which led to the Subway station, trying to force my mind to accept what I must regard as a demonstrated fact, when suddenly I stopped short. For I had asked myself a question which put a capstone of fantastic impossibility upon the whole affair.

If Gwendolen had murdered the doctor, or if she had seen him murdered before twenty-five minutes to twelve, *why in the world had she waited in that office until twenty minutes past?*

I threw out my hands with a gesture of despair. If the immutable laws of logic could lead to grotesque conclusions like this, I would prefer, I thought, to be mad.

Well, I would go and see Jeffrey. It was something to be thankful for, at least, that I could talk to him again, and quite frankly. I would own to him that the queer paradoxical position that he had maintained that night over the dinner table, the night we had read of Dr. Marshall's death in the newspaper, was the only sane one after all. The only certain knowledge was the inspired guess. The conclusions to which fact and reason led were insane, anyway.

XIII

Jeffrey Smokes a Pipe

It was about two hours later that I found a chance to make this confession to Jeffrey. He was in his own rooms when I arrived at the Atlas, and we went out to dinner together; then we came back to my quarters and settled down for a long talk.

He heard my story now with an attention close and serious enough to compensate for his lack of it before. He asked me to tell him everything that had happened since the night I had left his room and called in Mr. Stancliffe; and I was glad enough to comply with his request.

"And there we are," I concluded, when I had brought my narrative down to date. "She must have done it, or else have seen it done. And that's a conclusion which I find it utterly impossible to accept. I'm willing to give up all belief in evidence. I'll burn my book if you'll produce one of those inspired guesses of yours that will solve the riddle."

I was conscious when I spoke of a half-serious hope that he would, then and there, perform the miracle I had asked of him. At any rate I spoke gravely enough, being willing to risk the grin of derision with which he would, in all probability, greet my words.

But he answered as soberly as I had spoken. "Even if I had such a guess, it wouldn't do much good. We should have to build up to it with the plain brick and mortar of fact and inference before we could ask anyone else to accept our guess as anything but raving."

He ran his fingers through his hair, and then drummed with them on the table. Evidently he was as completely perplexed as I. Then he took up Mr. Stancliffe's note, which I had tossed across to him at an earlier stage of the conversation, and read it again.

"You have not seen Miss Carr since you left her that night out in Flatbush?" he asked presently.

I shook my head. "Nor heard from her," I added.

"You say you didn't get a good look at the man she thought was Pomeroy?"

"Nothing you could call a look," I answered. "But she seemed to have no doubt about him."

"And you've neither seen nor heard anything more, since this note, from Mr. Stancliffe?"

"Nothing whatever. I wish we had him here to talk to now. He's very clear headed."

"Yes," Jeffrey assented, "I wish so, too. He must be pretty busy with the clew he speaks of. He broke an appointment he had to pose for me this morning, broke it by telephone."

Neither of us spoke for a moment. Then he pushed back his chair and got to his feet.

"Haven't you a pipe somewhere, Drew?" he asked. "Mine are all at the studio, and cigarettes are no help in a puzzle like this. I want something to bite on."

"I don't know whether either of these will draw," said I, producing a couple, "but you are welcome to try."

My suspicion about them proved well founded. But a pipe was what he wanted, and after selecting the one that seemed the more promising, he methodically set himself about the unpleasant task of cleaning it.

"It's queer," said I, "the effect of association that smells have. It's so much stronger than sights or sounds. That pipe takes me straight back to Dr. Marshall's office. I told you how frightfully it smelled of stale tobacco."

He nodded absently.

"Miss Carr was speaking of the same thing to Stancliffe and me," I continued. "It was the night we took her up there. She said the office was a chamber of horrors to her, but it was the smell and not the sight of it that brought the whole thing back."

He could not have been listening, for he looked up now rather suddenly. "What's that?" he asked. "Say it again."

"It's not worth repeating."

But he was looking at me with a strange intensity. "Say it again," he commanded for the second time. "I want to be sure I understood you exactly."

So, feeling rather foolish, I began my little essay on the associative powers of smell again.

When I had finished, he threw down his pipe and literally clutched and tugged at his hair with both hands. His eyes were shining like coals.

"What in the world is the matter with you?" I asked.

"You were wanting an inspired guess a little while ago. Well, I've got one, that's all."

He sprang to his feet and began pacing excitedly up and down the room, plunging his hands into his pockets one minute, and pressing them against his head the next, as if he feared that something struggling in there would burst it.

"Drew, did you mean what you said?" he demanded, stopping in front of me and looking straight into my eyes. "Did you mean it? Are you willing to throw reason to the winds and take a leap in the dark? We may find we have wings, and we may not."

"I meant it absolutely," said I. "You can't produce a guess too fantastic for me to accept as a working hypothesis."

He nodded curtly, turned away, and resumed his patrol of the room. After a moment he stopped again. "Have you read today's papers?" he asked. "I haven't."

"Yes," said I. "Why?"

"It's all right, then," he answered, irrelevantly enough. "Nothing's happened to her yet."

"Happened to whom?"

"To *whom*?" he repeated. "To that poor girl out there alone in Flatbush. To Gwendolen Carr."

"You mean you think she is in actual physical danger?"

"Physical danger!" he shouted, catching the words out of my mouth. "She's in mortal peril tonight if anyone ever was."

Well, there was no denying that this was a guess. Whether it was inspired, or not, time alone would show. The inference of extreme peril to Miss Carr from the smell of stale tobacco from an old pipe was not a logical process at any rate.

Jeffrey's manner had quieted down rather suddenly. He was looking at his watch. "Well, it's only half past eight; that's one comfort," he said. "They go to bed early out in those parts, but there's still time. You have her telephone number, haven't you?"

"Somewhere in my pocketbook," said I, rummaging for the card. "What do you want me to tell her over the 'phone?"

"Tell her not to go to bed nor up to her own room. Tell her not to be alone in any room. She must have someone with her all the time until we come. And tell her we are coming as fast as an automobile can bring us. I'll order mine from the garage as soon as you've done talking to her."

I suppose my expression was still incredulous, for he came up to me and put his hand on my shoulder. "There isn't any time for explanations, really," he said. "It's life and death now. This question is going to be settled tonight, the whole of it; the Marshall mystery and all. But we must act first and think afterwards, if we are going to be in time."

His earnestness convinced me, although his reason did not.

Before I had got my connection with the telephone that I wanted in Flatbush, a good part of my belief in the validity of Jeffrey's guess had oozed away. It was one thing to stand, half spellbound, while he talked me into a decisive acceptance of his extraordinary theory; it was another thing to prepare to deliver the message he had intrusted to me into the mouthpiece of an unresponsive telephone.

I asked for Miss Carr. "She's not here," said the voice—a woman's—at the other end.

I told the voice who I was, hoping that with the knowledge, it would prove less uncommunicative. "But don't *you* know where she is?" the woman inquired, her voice showing symptoms of alarm. "I was hoping she had gone to see you. She disappeared about an hour ago, without a word to anybody. She hasn't been outside the house before in several days, and she certainly is not fit to be outside it now."

"Is she ill?"

"No. There is nothing the matter with her, except that I am afraid she is going crazy. For several days she's seemed afraid to go out of the house or be left alone, and in the night she wakes up screaming. But there is nothing you can call the matter. I tried to get her to have the doctor, but she wouldn't. She spoke of wishing to talk to you. That's why I thought maybe she had gone to see you now."

My further questions elicited nothing valuable in the way of additional information. I asked what Miss Carr had seemed afraid of, but it appeared that the landlady hadn't been able to make out. "Though," she added, "she couldn't have been more afraid if she had expected to be killed."

My heart felt like lead when I hung up that receiver and turned back to Jeffrey. "She's gone," said I hoarsely; "they don't know where she is. And, Jeffrey, for four days past, they say that she has been beside herself with terror—terror of death, they think. And, Jeffrey, how did you know? How could you have known? If it is an inspiration—you see I am ready to believe anything—why in God's name couldn't it have come before it was too late?"

Before he had time to answer me there came a ring at the bell.

"I hope that's Stancliffe," said I.

"Yes," said Jeffrey rather soberly, with an audible ring of excitement in his voice, "I hope so, too."

It was not Stancliffe whom we saw in the corridor when I flung my door wide open. But on seeing who it was, we both cried out together—Jeffrey and I—"Thank God!" For it was Gwendolen Carr herself.

I have a vague impression that the desk clerk was there beside her, half supporting her, and that he stammered out something apologetic for having brought the lady straight up, without announcing her in advance over the 'phone; but my 'phone had been busy for so long a time, and the lady seemed in haste.

At the time, however, neither Jeffrey nor I could spare enough attention from the girl in the doorway to give much thought to the desk clerk's apologies. She was very pale, and her eyes had in them that same wild, hunted look that I had seen there the night I had gone out to Flatbush after her.

For a minute or two, until we had got the door shut and had her seated in an easy chair, she managed to retain a superficial appearance of self-possession, thanked the desk clerk, said good evening to me, and bowed to Jeffrey when I pronounced their names—he had never seen her before, except at the inquest. But the moment it was possible for her to slacken the nervous tension which had driven her to undertake this journey and had supported her through it, she fairly broke down; struggled against her sobs for a moment, and then allowed the torrent to sweep her away.

I stood miserably by, trying to think of something to say or something to do, and from a sheer failure of mental resourcefulness did the best thing, the thing that Jeffrey was doing from another motive, namely, waited in silence for the torrent to spend itself.

When at last the sobs had given place to long tremulous breathing, Jeffrey flashed me a signal to the effect that he would do the talking himself. I was glad enough to have him, for I didn't know what to say myself.

"Can you listen while I tell you something?" he asked. "It's nothing you have to think about. All you have to do is to believe that it's true. We have just found out, Mr. Drew and I, that you have been in serious danger for the past few days. We know what the source of that danger is, and it's quite finally over now. All you have to do for the present is to believe that."

She had rapidly recovered her self-possession. "But I wasn't in any real danger," she said at last, "at least, not until today. Before that it was just—just dreams and fancies, and I think the mysteries and bewilderments that have beset me lately are enough to account for them."

"Never mind what it was; it's past now," said Jeffrey. "And the mysteries and bewilderments are over, too, or will be within a few hours—before morning, I hope. At any rate, we know who it was who killed Dr. Marshall."

I stared at him in stupefaction, and was about to utter an exclamation of astonishment, but he motioned to me to be silent. Then I saw, or thought I did, that he was telling her these things with the simple idea of calming her fears.

Gwendolen herself did not start at his words; if anything, her tired body relaxed a little deeper in the chair. She breathed a long sigh of infinite relief. Then she turned to me. "Does Jack—does Mr. Marshall know about it yet—know who it was who killed his father?"

"Not yet," said I. I was acutely miserable at having to take a part in a deception, which, though kindly meant, seemed bound to prove mere cruelty in the end.

Jeffrey, however, was perfectly at his ease, and he added: "We'll let you take the news around to him yourself presently." Then, after a moment's thought, he spoke again. "You came directly here from your boarding house in Flatbush, did you not, Miss Carr?"

"Yes," she said, "as directly as I could come."

"And had you any sort of misadventure on the way; anything that seemed like an accident?"

"Nothing at all."

"You didn't get the idea at any time that you were being followed?"

A quick alarm lighted up in her eyes, but she answered steadily enough, "No; not once."

Jeffrey drew a long breath of complete satisfaction. "It's perfectly incredible good luck," he said. Then he asked, rather irrelevantly it seemed to me: "What sort of person is your landlady? Can she keep her own counsel?"

Gwendolen smiled. "If she were told that it was for my good that she should do so, yes, for she is very fond of me."

"Where is the telephone in your house; out in one of the public rooms?"

"No, it is in a closet under the front stairs."

"Then," said Jeffrey quietly, "I'm going to get her on the 'phone and ask you to talk to her. You will tell her, if you please, that you are quite safe. Then find out if she has talked about your disappearance to anybody, especially to any of the boarders. Tell her to light up your room as if you were in it, and to tell anyone who asks about it that you are there. No, you needn't get up. I can put the 'phone on the arm of your chair, so."

During the five minutes that it took to carry out these rather singular instructions, Jeffrey paced slowly up and down the room, but more with the air of one who is merely waiting to put into effect the next move of his programme than of one trying to decide what his next move is to be.

I was looking at him in undisguised wonder, but his only reply to my look was a smile of anticipation and triumph. If he had lied to Gwendolen in saying that he knew who had killed Dr. Marshall, it was evident that he expected to make that lie the truth before any necessity for undeceiving her should arise.

When Gwendolen had finished her conversation with her landlady, she put the telephone over on my desk, and, rising, went over to another chair which permitted a less informal attitude. "I am sorry I made such a scene when I came in," she said. "I am quite right now, so you needn't feel that I must be handled like—something that might break or explode any minute. For these last few days I have thought I was awake when I was dreaming, and that I must be dreaming when I was awake. I couldn't tell which was which. If it had lasted much longer, I think it would have driven me mad. But it's over now. What is the next thing you want me to do?"

She asked the question of me, but did not seem surprised when Jeffrey answered it.

From the time when I had spoken of the odor of my pipe, I had been utterly unable to trace anything like continuity in his ideas. Well, he was arriving at the truth in his own way, and Heaven knew I had failed dismally enough to find it by mine!

But his capacity for surprising me seemed unlimited. When Gwendolen asked what we wanted her to do next, he dropped down comfortably into a big chair, as if there were no hurry in the world, and said: "I'd like to hear something about those dreams of yours when you seemed to be awake, and the waking things that seemed as if they must be dreams."

"It is a little hard to talk about," she said. "You see, I haven't really slept much since the inquest—since that evening when Mr. Marshall came up to see me."

"Do the dreams go back as far as that?"

"No, those first nights were just simply wide awake. There was nothing terrifying about them. The first of the dreams came the night you took me home—she turned to me as she said it—the night we met Pomeroy on the sidewalk, or I thought we did, at any rate."

"That was the night you thought you were going to sleep," I observed.

"I remember. Perhaps the whole thing is just a judgment upon me for having boasted to you and Mr. Stancliffe that I meant to get off that night without a bromide."

"You spoke a minute ago," Jeffrey remarked, "as if you doubted whether the man you passed on the sidewalk was actually Pomeroy. You were quite sure of it at the time, weren't you?"

"That's where the puzzle begins," she said. "I don't know whether he belongs with the dreams or the realities."

"You've seen him more than that once?"

"Yes," she said. "Not again that night, but every night since then."

"You saw him at night? Where did you see him? Was he going by on the sidewalk, or did you see him in the yard?" It was I who asked this question, and it brought a most astonishing answer.

"He wasn't outdoors at all. He was in my room."

"Have you seen anyone else in your room besides Pomeroy?" Jeffrey asked. It might have been the most matter-of-fact question in the world, from the tone of his voice.

She hesitated a little over the answer. "It makes me think I am losing my wits just to talk about it," she said. "I've seen Dr. Marshall, too."

"In your room, just as Pomeroy was?"

"Yes."

"More than once?"

"Every night after that first night—after the night I saw Mr. Pomeroy outdoors, I mean."

"What did they do when you saw them, Pomeroy and Dr. Marshall, I mean?"

It was marvelous to me the way he kept his voice from showing the strange mysterious thrill which her words must have caused him. Whatever he felt, his tone expressed nothing but a keen, common-sense interest.

"They didn't do anything," she said. "I would be lying there in bed wide awake—feeling sure that I was wide awake—trying to keep my mind down to sensible, everyday things, and then, suddenly, I would see one of them standing there in the room."

"What light did you see them by?"

"There is a big arc lamp on the corner that shines in through my window and makes a patch of bright light in the middle of the room. It's there he would be standing, whichever one he was. And then I would cry out and wake myself up, only it wouldn't feel like waking up, except that the thing I had seen would vanish. But it still left me feeling as if I had been awake all the time."

There was a little silence after that, but before either of us spoke, she went on again, of her own accord. "Of course it's easy in the morning—it has been, that is, until today—to say that I've just been having nightmares, and that there is nothing to make a fuss about. But when night comes round again, and when you know you're awake—know it as well as I know it now—"

"You still went on taking your bromides, I suppose," said Jeffrey.

"Yes, one every night, but they didn't do me any good; they didn't even make me feel sleepy."

"You never took a second one when you thought the first one had failed to have any effect?"

"No, never."

"Why not?"

"The doctor who gave them to me—the doctor out there in Flatbush—told me it would be dangerous to take more than one. Oh—it wasn't for myself that I cared. There hasn't been a night when I didn't feel a temptation to take them all at once and go to sleep anyway. Whether I ever woke up or not, didn't seem to matter—not to me, that is. But I've kept saying to myself that I mustn't run any risks; that if I were to die now, especially in some such way as that, with all that you and Mr. Stancliffe know pointing straight against me, it would be too terrible for him—for—"

She was not able to complete the sentence, but I could have done it for her. I saw what she meant, and again I marveled at her courage. If she were to die—die of an overdose of sleeping powders, no power in the world could ever convince her lover that she was not his father's murderess.

There was no expression in Jeffrey's face at all, save of the most concentrated thought. But now he said an exceedingly curious thing. "You haven't taken all the powders yet, Miss Carr, have you? You must have one or two left."

"One," she said, looking at him wide eyed.

He drew in a long breath and expelled it violently, as a man might who had just had a narrow escape from something.

"In the natural course of things," he said, "I suppose you would have taken that tonight?"

"Yes, I suppose so."

"Some of your landlady's boarders are more or less transient, I presume," he said; "a new one or two coming in every few days?"

"Yes."

"There are one or two of them who just have rooms, who take their meals elsewhere?"

"Yes."

"You said something a few minutes ago, to the effect that until today it had been easy to be sure during the daytime that you had suffered from nothing but bad dreams. What happened today that seemed to mix up dreams and reality more than they were mixed already?"

"My room has a hardwood floor," she said, "and this morning when the light fell across it slantwise—quite early this morning, before I had gone down to breakfast, I saw a print there on the floor—right where I had seen the ghost standing in the night, and I got up and looked at it. It was the imprint of the heel of a man's rubber, showing the crisscross marks that keep you from slipping—a new rubber; but it had been a little damp and a little dirty, and had left a mark. And the mark was not there the night before."

XIV

And Tries an Experiment

I think that is all there is to tell," she concluded after a little silence. "When I saw that mark on the floor, I didn't know whether I was mad or not, for a dream or a ghost could not leave a mark. Yet the print I saw there was the print of Dr. Marshall's foot. I had seen him standing there in my room just as plainly as I saw him that day in the office. I've been torturing myself with that all day. I didn't want a doctor. I knew what he'd think well enough. But I thought if I could talk to you and Mr. Stancliffe, perhaps you could do something; perhaps you would tell me whether I was mad or not, anyway."

Jeffrey got up and looked at his watch. "I am going out for a few minutes," he said, "but I'll be back directly. In the meantime, remember the first thing I said to you when you came in here. You have been, during these last few days, in a very real and tangible danger. The danger is over now because we understand what it is. We've learned the source of it. As regards being mad, don't worry about that. You are saner than I am, or than most people are. You've shown yourself to be one of the sanest and one of the bravest people I know of. Now don't worry."

He went out without another word, and a moment later I heard the door of his apartment close behind him. I guessed that he wanted to telephone, and did not care to take us into his confidence just then regarding the message he was going to send.

The moment he had gone, Gwendolen turned to me. "Must I wait any longer?" she asked. "Can't you trust me with the whole story now? It's all very well to be told not to worry, and that it's coming out all right—I believe it is—but if you know—"

"I don't know," said I. "I am as much in the dark as you are. The curious thing about it is that Jeffrey himself didn't know when we sat down in this room to talk it over after dinner. And then, suddenly, he just guessed. My mind isn't like Jeffrey's or Mr. Stancliffe's; it can't fly. It can only go straight ahead, a step at a time. I imagine Mr. Stancliffe sees something—the same thing that Jeffrey does. He wrote to me three or four days ago about having a clew which he was working on. I haven't seen or heard from him since, but I am pretty sure of this, that between them they'll solve it. Jeffrey told me, just before you came in, that it would be solved tonight. I know he means it. He isn't the sort to talk idly."

She leaned back in her chair, her eyelids drooped lower and lower, and her hands lay inert in her lap. "I'm so tired," she said, "that I'd just like to stop altogether and never go on again. Did you ever feel like that?"

It was then that I had a really good idea. "How long is it," I asked, "since you have had anything to eat—since you've really eaten anything, I mean?"

"I don't know," she said; "I really don't remember, but I do know that food would choke me now."

I reached for the telephone, nevertheless, and ordered an eggnog and a sandwich. "You needn't taste either of them when they come, unless they look good to you," said I.

They arrived just as Jeffrey was returning. "Good for you, Drew," he said, noticing the contents of the tray. "We ought to have done that long ago."

Gwendolen was still inclined to be rebellious.

"If you'll eat it all," said Jeffrey, "you shall have some good news; but not until after the last swallow and the last bite."

Once she got started, it required no urging to make her continue. "I wonder why girls are always so silly about that," she observed. "We get into a dreadful state of mind and think we are going to die of all sorts of complicated emotions, when the only thing the matter with us is that we are hungry."

She drank the last of the yellow liquid in the tall glass, and then turned to Jeffrey. "Now have I earned my good news?"

"I've been talking to Mrs. Marshall over the telephone," Jeffrey said, "and she's coming straight here. She's on her way now. She says that Jack is a great deal better—so much better that she's had a talk with him about the whole affair, the first one since the murder was committed."

Gwendolen pressed her lips together tightly. "I suppose she wants to hear all that I can tell her," she said. "Well, I'll do my best."

"That's not what she's coming for," Jeffrey said. "She already knows all you can tell her, and more, too. She's coming to take you home with her. Mr. Drew and I are going out to Flatbush tonight, and we are going to spend the night in your room, or as much of the night as may be necessary. We mean to catch the ghost, Miss Carr. I expect he will prove solid enough. By the way, do you mind sitting down and writing a little note to your landlady, telling her that we're all right and she's to do what we say?"

"It *was* real, then?" she asked. "A real man who got into my room and stood there glaring at me? But if he was real and wanted to kill me, why didn't he do it when he had the chance?"

"Never mind that," said Jeffrey easily. "You'll know in good time."

Before she had finished writing the note, Madeline arrived. The two women had hardly seen each other before, since Madeline, on the day of the inquest, had been heavily veiled, and had had no idea that the young girl who took the stand as the last person known to have seen Dr. Marshall alive would ever cross her path again. And while Madeline stood there looking across the room at this young girl, whose life story she had just heard, for the first time, from Jack's lips—as she stood there looking at her, I looked at Madeline herself. I saw the color come up into her cheeks and a softer brightness, the brightness of tears, come into her eyes. I had never seen just that look in Madeline's face before. I knew now what it was that I had always missed there.

Then she held out her hands to Gwendolen. "You poor dear child," she said unsteadily; "you poor dear pair of children, you and Jack." She crossed the room impulsively, and took the girl in her arms and kissed her. "But you are going to be happy now," she said, "you two. Trust us for that." Then she looked over her shoulder at me. "Can I take her now, Clifford, this instant?"

"You'll have to ask Jeffrey," said I. "He's running the show."

"We'll leave it to her," he said. "Miss Carr, do you feel equal to having an experiment tried on you?"

"Not tonight, Mr. Jeffrey," protested Madeline. "Wait until tomorrow for whatever it is."

"I don't think it will be very painful," said Jeffrey; "at least it will soon be over. If you feel equal to letting me try it tonight, then tomorrow morning at breakfast I think I can guarantee you the whole story complete."

"But it isn't necessary," said Madeline; "it can't be necessary. Won't tomorrow morning do just as well?"

"I don't know just what you mean by trying an experiment on me," Gwendolen said thoughtfully, "but I shan't mind anything, even though it is painful, that will help solve our problem, or that will make the complete solution come any quicker than it otherwise would. But"—

she hesitated—"there isn't any doubt about what you told me, is there? You do know, don't you, who it was that killed Jack's father?"

"No, there is no doubt about that," said Jeffrey quietly. "I don't think you will find the experiment painful. I want you merely to come across the hall to my quarters to see if you recognize something that I shall show you."

Madeline seemed half minded to make some further protest against the plan, but apparently she thought better of it, for she drew the young girl's arm through her own, and turned to Jeffrey. "All right, then," said she. "The sooner the better. We're ready."

"I'm not an orderly person like Mr. Drew," he said, "so my things are all higgledy-piggledy."

He led the way out into the corridor, unlocked his own door and preceded us into his quarters, touching a wall button, which flooded the room with light, as he did so.

"Sit down somewhere," he said, "all of you. It won't take me but a minute to find the thing I want, or at least I hope it won't."

He opened his escritoire as he spoke, and began rummaging among the riotous disorder of incongruous articles which were shut up within.

It was while he was so occupied that I made a discovery which caused me acute embarrassment, and not a little annoyance. Laid out in a row on the center table, the most conspicuous thing in the room, was a complete set of the plaster casts which Jeffrey had had taken from Dr. Marshall's hands only a few days before the murder. It seemed horribly inconsiderate of Jeffrey to have brought her in here where they were. If it should occur to her to ask whose hands they were, or if there should be anything about to enable her to make the discovery for herself, they would prove about as grisly a reminder of her frightful experience as could well have been contrived.

When I reflected what her occupation was, or had been up to a few days ago, when I remembered the little glass table in the corner of the barber shop in the St. Anthony Hotel, it seemed to me more than likely that she would be able to identify those hands, just by looking at them, without asking a single question.

I did what I could to divert her attention from them by attracting it to other objects about the room, the Japanese prints on the wall, and so on, and I tried, vainly however, to catch Madeline's eye and enlist her assistance. But her attention seemed fixed upon Jeffrey as he bent over his writing desk and pulled out one drawer after another, only to shut it again, with a bang, after tumbling over its contents with his impatient fingers.

Presently I saw that my efforts at diversion had been of no avail. The moment Gwendolen's eye fell on those white plaster hands, they drew her like a magnet. She left her chair and stood over the table where they lay, gazing at them as if they had fascinated her. "Aren't they beautiful," she said after a while, glancing up at me.

"They're considered so, I believe," said I. How I wished that Jeffrey would hurry up and find the thing he was looking for in the desk. In vain I signaled Madeline to do something to create a diversion.

"They're all the same pair of hands," the girl remarked at length, "although they are in different positions. So they can't be from a statue. They must have been made from a live man. Have you any idea whose they are, Mr. Drew?"

"I haven't an idea," I stammered.

"What's that?" said Jeffrey from the desk, speaking in his most casual tone. "Didn't I tell you about them? I thought I had. They are Dr. Marshall's."

For an instant I mentally accused him of the most utterly inhuman want of tact I'd ever encountered. The next instant I saw my mistake; saw that the article he pretended to be searching for in his desk was a pure fiction. That the real experiment connected itself somehow with those hands. It was rather cruel, I thought, but not inconsiderate.

The effect of his words on the girl was most surprising. She did not shrink, nor turn pale. She colored a little instead, and her eyes sparkled, as if with anger.

"Don't you trust me, after all?" she asked. "Why are you trying to play me a trick? These are not Dr. Marshall's hands."

"How do you know?" Jeffrey asked.

"Because hands are the only thing I *do* know. A hand is as individual to me as a face. I work on them from morning till night. They are the first part of a person that I see. I watched Dr. Marshall's for more than an hour that terrible day in his office. Do you think I could forget them?"

Jeffrey seemed to find it hard to control his voice, but he still did his best to make it sound casual and commonplace. "Can you tell me," he asked, "how those hands that you are talking about were different from these on the table?"

"Why, they were larger," she said. "They would need a glove a full size larger than these. They were beautiful hands, too, but quite different from these in every way. The fingers were more pointed and the nails more almond shaped. And, then, the middle fingers of Dr. Marshall's hands were longer. The whole hand, when the fingers weren't stretched apart, made an oval."

Jeffrey's eyes were blazing now, and his color was as high as hers. When he spoke again his voice was trembling with an excitement which the utmost repression could not conceal.

"Miss Carr," he said, "these casts here on the table were made, in my presence, from Dr. Marshall's hands. If you doubt my words, Mrs. Marshall here will tell you that what I say is true."

Suddenly I saw that the girl was trembling violently, and that every particle of color had receded from her face. She swayed a little where she stood. Madeline saw it, too, and going quickly up to her, put a strong arm about her.

Jeffrey had hesitated an instant. Now he went on again. "But, nevertheless, Miss Carr, you are not mistaken, or, at least, only partly. For these are not the hands of the man who sat behind the desk in Dr. Marshall's office when you talked to him that day. They are not the hands of the man who made that wanton and brutal attack upon you. For when the bell rang that summoned you into his office, Dr. Marshall was already dead! *And the man you talked with was his murderer!*"

XV

Mr. Stancliffe Bids Us Good Evening

Jeffrey must have accomplished a good deal during his brief absence from my quarters, when I supposed he had gone to telephone, for when we emerged together from the great doorway of the Atlas, we found his motor car drawn up to the curb behind Madeline's brougham.

When we had put the ladies into the latter vehicle, I observed that there were two men in the touring car. The chauffeur would account for one, but who could the other be? Jeffrey introduced him as Lieutenant Richards, and then climbed, himself, into the driver's seat, motioning the chauffeur to take the one beside him. That meant that the stranger and I were to occupy the tonneau. I would have liked that seat beside Jeffrey myself, for I was bursting with questions. But it was evident that he did not want to answer them yet, for his manner of seating us in the car was obviously the result of forethought; and after conquering a momentary pique, I realized clearly that, with grave problems still ahead of him, my friend was right in not wishing to be bothered with those he had already solved.

My companion in the tonneau proved more entertaining than I had at first expected to find him. He had been a member of the New York detective force for a good many years, and had a string of stories to tell, which would have fascinated me had not the particular story we were actually living in, and whose solution still remained to be accomplished, made them sound rather tame. The most interesting thing I learned from him was that he and Jeffrey were old friends. In his newspaper and police court days, my oddly inspired artist friend had been a familiar figure in the "Front Office," and the police had often put his guesses to good use.

When we were crossing the Williamsburg Bridge Jeffrey, with a nod of his head, interrupted our conversation, and summoned us to a council of war. First of all he inquired particularly of me about the location of the house in Flatbush.

"Now," said he, when he was satisfied that he understood, "this isn't a raid we're making. It's a surprise, and, consequently, we can't go chugging right up to the door in this car. We'll stop when we're about three or four blocks away, and I'll go up to the house on foot. We don't know whether our man is in the house or out of it, so we'll have to find out how the land lies before we can set out about the business."

Then Richards made a suggestion. "If your friend happens not to be in the house, happens to be on the way there, and comes upon this car with three men in it, waiting at a lonely corner, don't you think he'll be likely to smell something more than gasoline?"

"Right," said Jeffrey. "When we get there, I will slow down and drop off at the corner, and then Charles here can drive for ten minutes straight on down the avenue. Then he can turn around and come back. If you don't find me waiting there on the corner, then drive straight on for five minutes more, and come back again."

He gave his whole attention to the steering wheel after that. The lieutenant and I fell silent, too. I think that even this veteran, who had had so many such adventures as the one we had now set out upon, felt a little thrill of excitement over the prospect that was before us. In my own veins I felt it mounting higher and higher with every mile which the flying car devoured between us and our destination.

We carried out our programme to the letter. The chauffeur slid into Jeffrey's seat, slowed down, and Jeffrey dropped off at the corner, where my pointing finger indicated. Then, for as long a ten minutes as I ever spent, we drove straight away from the scene which was to witness the solution of our mystery.

But we were not forced to repeat the maneuver and waste an interminable five minutes more going in the opposite direction, for on coming back to the corner again we saw Jeffrey nod to us from the shadow.

"Drive off," he said to the chauffeur, as soon as the lieutenant and I had scrambled out, "and keep driving. Don't come near here for an hour. After that I think it will be safe enough for you to wait here for us."

He set a brisk pace up the lonely, ill-lighted street where Gwendolen and I had walked less than a week before. "I think it's all right," he said presently, in a tone barely above a whisper. "He went out about five o'clock and hasn't come back yet. He generally comes in late, the landlady tells me. But I imagine, unless he suspects something, he won't be much longer now."

The thing which now seemed most likely to cause a mishap to our plans was the possibility that "he," whoever he was, might see us in the act of walking toward the boarding house, if not of actually entering it. The sight of the three of us at that time of night would be likely to suggest a good many disquieting things to a guilty conscience. The thought of this possibility made it hard to keep down to the unhurried, though still rapid, pace which Jeffrey was setting.

The front door swung open the moment we set foot on the steps; in this particular, at least, the reconnoissance our scout had made was not in vain. Five seconds later it closed behind us.

Jeffrey directed a swift glance of inquiry toward the stout, shapeless, middle-aged woman, whose hand was still on the door knob. She was not beautiful, with her tear-reddened eyes and her worried expression; particularly not as our visit had evidently interrupted her preparations for bed, which a hurriedly assumed tea gown was quite inadequate to hide. But she proved an efficient ally for all that.

She understood Jeffrey's glance without a word. "No," she said; "not yet."

"We're all right so far then, I think," my friend whispered. "Is the light still burning in Miss Carr's room, and are the shades drawn down tight?"

"Everything's just as you ordered it."

"In that case there's nothing more for you to bother about. You'd better go back to bed and try to get some sleep. It may be hours before anything happens. Pretend to anyway, even if you think you can't; he mustn't see anything about the house that will strike him as unusual. Come along";—this he addressed to us—"he may be turning up at any minute now."

He led the way up to Gwendolen's room without another word. It was on the third story, and at the back of the house. The stairway which led from the second floor to the third story was simply a continuation of the back stairs from the first floor to the second. There were two closed doors at the stair head, but the light which came through the crack under one of them told us which room was Gwendolen's.

Jeffrey opened it and motioned us to go in. Richards and I both started to obey his signal, and then, at the same moment, started back again, for both of us thought we saw a figure, well covered with blankets, there in the bed.

"It's all right," Jeffrey whispered; "there's nothing there but a dummy. Our landlady has done a good job."

He, however, did not follow us into the room, but remained on the landing between the two doors.

I could see that he was puzzled about something. "Anything wrong?" I asked.

"I don't think so, but I can't quite figure this out. This other door opens into an attic. His room's at the foot of the stairs here on the floor below, and this straight, narrow stairway makes the place a perfect rat trap."

"Well," said Richards, "if it's a rat trap, we may as well use it to catch our rat."

"What do you mean?"

"Why, we were planning to grab him when he came in, but this room may not be as dark as we could wish. He may see us, and turn around and bolt. But there's a little niche just past the foot of the stairs that's as dark as a pocket. I can wait down there until he opens his door and starts to come up. Then I can close in on the foot of the stairs here, and we'll have him sure."

Jeffrey frowned thoughtfully and ruffled his hair. "Well, that sounds like sense," he said at last. "You'd better do it."

All of us had our shoes off by this time, and the lieutenant vanished from the room as noiselessly as if he had been a ghost himself. Then Jeffrey took a final survey of the room.

It was too plain and prosaic a little place to be worthy of particular description. A white iron bed stood in one corner, with a small table beside it, and a washstand a little farther along, while against the opposite wall stood an ordinary oak bureau between two gas jets, one of them lighted.

Jeffrey closed the door, and whispered to me to put out the light. "Only be careful," he urged, "not to let your shadow fall on that window shade; that might spoil the whole thing. It's not at all unlikely that, at this very moment, he's watching that oblong patch of light and waiting for it to disappear before he comes into the house."

When I had turned out the light, he himself raised the shade and opened the window a little, standing off to the side, however, in order not to risk exposing himself to the view of the keen-eyed watcher, who might be waiting somewhere out there in the dark.

When the shade was raised and the bluish-white rays of the big arc lamp on the corner cast their patch of light on the floor, the room was not, as Richards had foreseen, as dark as we could wish. The reflection from that spot on the floor diffused a soft light through the small room, in which, though we chose the darkest corners, we could hardly hope to remain invisible. Jeffrey, however, soon thought of an expedient to remedy this difficulty. There was a square of dark-colored carpet on the floor beside the bed, and this he dragged out over the patch of light upon the floor. It absorbed the rays, instead of reflecting them, and darkened the room appreciably.

Each of us took one of the small, straight chairs with which the room was furnished, and sat down there in the dark to wait.

In confirmation of my friend's theory, that a pair of watchful eyes had been turned on that translucent window shade waiting for the light behind it to disappear, it was not more than five minutes after the light had been put out before we heard the click of a latchkey in the street door.

The newcomer let himself in, closed the door behind him, walked up the front stairs and down the hall to his room at the foot of the second stairway. He did it all quietly, but not in the least stealthily, did it, in short, so exactly in the manner of any ordinary boarder coming home late, that I felt a momentary incredulity as to his being the man we were waiting for. Well, so far he was only doing a perfectly plain, law-abiding act; he had no need of silence.

I heard a whisper from Jeffrey, so low that it barely reached my ears, "All's right so far; he's got past Richards in the lower hall."

I dared not risk an answer. The thing we were waiting for—whatever the exact form it might happen to take—could be expected to materialize now at any moment.

It was not until we looked at our watches afterwards that I had any idea how long, in hours and minutes, that wait lasted. It seemed perfectly interminable, not only as if it never would end, but as if, somehow, it had never begun. If only that had been moonlight on the floor instead of the rays from the fixed lamp on the corner, its moving shadow would have given us some clew. As it was, the swift procession of my thoughts was all that served to mark time. Perhaps I should have said rout rather than procession, for no effort of will that I could make in those strange circumstances would serve to bring them under orderly discipline.

I may confess that as the time stretched out, longer and longer, I began to experience a perfectly irrational impulse of panic, the feeling that I must do something, even if it were only to shout aloud, to break that uncanny spell of silence and of mystery.

I had expected, and I think Jeffrey shared the belief with me, that some faint sound would give us warning in advance of the arrival of the man we were waiting for, something that would give us time to get to our feet and poise our bodies for a spring upon the intruder who was to appear.

A warning came, indeed, but not until it was too late to hazard the slightest movement. And it was not a sound at all; it was just a puff of cool air upon our faces. The door must have opened, but it had opened soundlessly.

I strained my eyes toward it, but saw nothing, nothing at all, unless that shapeless area of blacker darkness than the rest of the room could be called something to see.

My eyes were riveted on the place where I knew the door was, and I was still waiting to see someone come in through it—some human person, moving stealthily, no doubt, but in a human way, and with some faintly discernible sound.

And then, I don't know why, I looked at the patch of light in the middle of the room.

It was not self-control that kept me from screaming at the sight I saw there! It was simply the total paralysis of nightmare. I could not have uttered a cry to save my life. I could not even gasp, and I am sure that for a full second my heart literally stood still.

There, with the full white light from the street lamp outside shining upon it, was the face, nothing but the face, of the man who had been murdered two weeks before in an uptown office building in New York! The face of a man I had often seen and talked with.

But I had never seen it look like that, for it looked now like the dead face of a man who had been murdered. The flesh, where the short dark beard he wore afforded a view of it, was a perfectly dead, colorless white. The eyeballs protruded, sightless and expressionless, reflecting the light that shone upon them, but dully. The jaw hung perfectly slack, and the tongue was lolling out of the open mouth.

For a while—ten seconds, I suppose—it remained perfectly lifeless, perfectly motionless. During that time I could no more have commanded a voluntary motion of my body than if I had been carved in marble.

And then very slowly over that ghastly face came an indescribable change. Very, very gradually I saw it come back to life; saw the eyes light up with the activity of a living brain behind them; saw the lips draw into a sinister sort of grin, which, though cruel and formidable, was human. What I was looking at was no longer a dead mask of unspeakable horror, but the face of a living man.

The eyes narrowed suddenly and began shifting swiftly, furtively around the room. The face, which was all that had been visible at any time, made a sudden move toward the bed—

And vanished.

I caught a fleeting glimpse of that same irregular shape of deeper blackness than the shadows about the doorway.

I heard Jeffrey, with an oath, spring to his feet, and then I heard a door slam. In less than a second Jeffrey had pulled an electric torch from his pocket, and its faint light made us visible to each other, but we were alone in the room.

His face was white and clammy with sweat, and his hands were shaking so that he could hardly hold the torch. For myself, I was conscious of feeling the way he looked.

I was the first to reach the door, and flung it open. "Richards!" I shouted. "Look out below!" I don't think there could have been more than three or four seconds between the vanishing of that face and the ring of my shout down the stairway.

We half ran, half fell down the stairs, only to find ourselves facing the glare of the lieutenant's bull's-eye, while our own torch revealed nothing but a look of utter bewilderment in his face.

"What are you doing here!" Jeffrey cried. "Have you let him give you the slip?"

Richards's face, if possible, looked more astonished than ever. "But he hasn't come out of his room at all," he answered.

"What do you mean?"

"Just that. I've never had my eyes off his door since he went inside. He locked it after he went in, and then his light went out. I tell you that door hasn't opened since he shut it and locked it behind himself."

Thought is, of course, infinitely quicker than the possibility of expressing it. For an instant I half believed that I had really slept; that the vision and the paralysis of nightmare which accompanied it had, indeed, been a dream; that some passing gust of the night air had opened that silent door and then slammed it shut again.

Jeffrey's mind had been working as fast, but in another and more profitable direction. "I was a fool," he whispered. "I might have known he wouldn't use the stairs. Break down the door!"

The lieutenant looked dubious for a moment, and then something in Jeffrey's manner convinced him. Bracing himself against the wall at the opposite side of the passage, he drove his heel, with shattering force, against the door. The blow was well placed, right over the lock, and there was no need of a second. The door swung slowly open, and we rushed in.

There was a faint light in the room from a single gas jet, turned low. Standing before the bureau, with his back to us, was a man clad in a long, hooded robe, or domino, of black silk. I remember now, though I did not notice it at the time, that he was in the act of setting an empty glass upon the marble top of the bureau, when I first saw him.

"Stand where you are!" cried the lieutenant. "Don't move, on your life!"

But his words might have fallen on deaf ears, for all the effect they had. The man picked up a towel from the bureau top, buried his face in it, wiped it, in fact, as if he had just been washing.

When the operation was completed, he turned for the first time, and looked up at us. "I shall make no resistance," he said quietly. "You needn't worry." He had spoken, but no voice had come with the words—only a whisper.

The face that I stood looking into was the face of Carlton Stancliffe!

"Lieutenant," said Jeffrey, with a thrill of triumph in his voice, "permit me to make you acquainted with James Hyde, M.D., formerly of New York, latterly of Australia, and last of all of the stage. He merits your close attention and your watchful care, for he is the murderer of his former friend and colleague, Dr. Roscoe Marshall."

The lieutenant was most businesslike. He pulled out of his pocket a pair of handcuffs. "I know you said you didn't intend to resist," he observed, "but I'll feel better leaving you with these on your wrists while I go to telephone for a patrol wagon."

Meanwhile, Jeffrey, with a touch on my arm, drew my attention to the ceiling of the room. There was an opening in it up into the attic above. "That's his route, you will observe," he said. "Evidently when the house was built the attics weren't finished off, and this was the only way of getting into them. It provided him with exactly the thing he needed. I noticed that he had oiled the hinges of the door leading into Miss Carr's room. If I had examined those on the other door, up at the head of the stairs, I shouldn't have made the mistake of supposing that he used the stairs at all. It's only an easy spring, you see, from the table up through the trap, and he could be still more expeditious about coming back. By the time the girl's screams had aroused the house, he'd be back in his own room, ready, if he chose, to unlock his door ostentatiously, and inquire what the matter was."

"There's one thing we mustn't forget," he added, "and I think I'll go upstairs for it now. That's the last one of that packet of powders, the one she would have taken tonight—the one that would have sent her off into a sleep from which there is no wakening, if she had taken it."

The lieutenant was about to leave the room in search of the telephone. "I can spare you gentlemen both those errands," said Mr. Stancliffe, in his whisper. "You will not be able to find that paper of powders upstairs, for the simple reason that I have just taken them myself. And for that same reason, it will be unnecessary to telephone for a patrol wagon. The coroner is the man you want to talk to. I shall be dead in ten minutes."

"The doctor, quick!" cried Jeffrey.

The lieutenant left the room with a rush, met the landlady in the hall, and got the telephone number of the nearest local practitioner almost before he had time to ask for it. She was an efficient woman, that landlady.

Mr. Stancliffe sat down comfortably enough on the edge of his bed, stretching his manacled arms up above his head to their utmost reach. Then he relaxed and lay down quietly, as if composing himself for sleep. "It's absolutely no use calling up a doctor," he said. "I shall be beyond his reach before he gets here."

Then he turned to us and smiled the faintly contemptuous smile of a man who lays down his cards at the end of an unprofitable game. "I will confess," he said, "I didn't expect my riddle to be solved. I thought the world had grown too stupid. On the whole I am not sorry to know that there will be a little leaven of intelligence left in it when I am gone. I don't know which one of you two young men possesses it. I am sorry I cannot hope to wait to clear up any little points about my mystery with regard to which you may still be in doubt."

His whisper had been growing fainter and fainter. Now it was barely audible at all—"Already—I—find—I—am—going. Good evening—gentlemen."

XVI

Jeffrey Explains

Mr. Stancliffe was not actually dead when the doctor, summoned by Richards in such hot haste, arrived.

"There is probably no hope in the world," that gentleman had said, "but there's no doubt of our duty to attempt to revive him." So for the next half hour he did everything that skill and energy could suggest, and kept Jeffrey and me pretty busy following out his instructions. Finally, however, he turned away.

"That's all I can do, gentlemen," he said, "except to notify the coroner. Your testimony will doubtless be wanted at the inquest."

While this had been going on Richards was busily occupied in a careful, systematic search through the dead man's effects. It was all very well for Jeffrey to proclaim Carlton Stancliffe as the murderer of Dr. Marshall, but it would be a little better to have some sort of corroborative evidence to back it up with.

The wardrobe and the bureau drawers were empty, but a great many articles were lying about the room; a big trunk was half packed with others, and an empty suit case yawned to receive its share. A little hanging shelf full of books was the only thing in the room that gave it an air of habitation.

Richards finished his investigations at the trunk just about the time the doctor went away. "I don't find anything here, Mr. Jeffrey, that bears out your theory," he said.

"No," my friend said coolly, "I didn't think you would."

He himself was standing with his hands in his pockets gazing at the little row of well-worn books on the shelf.

"I suppose," said Richards, half in sarcasm, but half in uneasy earnest, "I suppose *you* know where everything important in this room is without looking."

"Yes," my friend said quietly, "I do. One of them, unless I am greatly mistaken, is in one of the dead man's trousers pockets."

He did not turn his head as he spoke, but remained in his former position, running his eye along the titles of the volumes that comprised Mr. Stancliffe's little library. Richards eyed him doubtfully, half inclined to think my friend was making game of him; then he thought better of it, went over to the bed, and bent down over the body that lay there.

"Is this what you mean?" I heard him ask; "something wrapped up in oiled silk?"

"That's it," said Jeffrey.

The lieutenant turned around to the light and unwrapped the little package. It was a very small hypodermic syringe with a broken needle in it.

"Smell of it," commanded Jeffrey still without turning around. The lieutenant sniffed obediently.

"Hmm, tobacco," he said.

"Nicotine," Jeffrey corrected, "pure nicotine. And that little syringe in your hand is the instrument with which he committed the murder."

"Well," said Richards with a sigh, "*I* don't know how you do it. Is there anything else you can direct me to?"

"Why," said Jeffrey, "besides those wigs and make-up boxes on the bureau, I think the only other thing of importance is this," and he put out his hand and drew a book from the shelf. It was bound in well-worn black leather and had a half-obliterated monogram on the back—"J. R. M."

"Look here, Drew," he said, "this ought to take us pretty close to the Grosvenor Building tragedy."

He opened it and began turning the pages backward; the last ones were all blank.

"What's the book?" I asked.

"Dr. Marshall's case book," said he, "and the last entry he made ought to prove interesting." The next moment he found it. The page was only about one third filled with Dr. Marshall's fine, upright, precise handwriting.

"Stancliffe—Carlton," it read. "His third visit this week. Shows more clearly than before the symptoms of degenerative, recurrent hypomania. If the examination bears this out I shall take steps to have him put under restraint. Still perfectly sane in the legal sense, but distinctly dangerous at large."

"Well," said I thoughtfully, "he was right up to the last, wasn't he?"

Jeffrey shivered. "No," said he, "it was his one great mistake. He ought to have acted sooner." And then he repeated half under his breath: "'Third visit this week.'"

He closed the book and handed it to the lieutenant.

"I think," said he, "that my friend and I here have had about enough. If we can't do anything more for you we'll be off. I doubt if there's anything else to find."

Jeffrey emptied his glass and took a long pull at my pipe, the pipe he had set about cleaning so few hours before—the pipe that had so unexpectedly provided him with the clew to our mystery. I had already made him a present of it.

"Well," said he, "it's four o'clock in the morning. Do you want to go to bed like an only moderately disreputable citizen, or shall we make a night of it, thrashing out the whole tale?"

"You know what I want, well enough," said I. "When you took the driver's seat in the automobile coming home and brought me all the way up here without a word of explanation, I began to wonder whether you ever meant to talk or not; whether you weren't going to leave me to wallow in my ignorance and stupidity to my dying day."

"I had to get my story in order before I could tell it to you," said he. "I knew there would be no use showing you my kite until I had tied a tail of reasonable inferences on behind it."

Really, I believe he had postponed telling his story until now for the purpose of providing us with a reasonable excuse for not going to bed when we did get home.

I may as well preface the narrative with which Jeffrey was about to favor me with the remark that in one particular he had made a mistake. A further search of Stancliffe's effects revealed one more article of capital importance, a remarkable diary in the handwriting of the murderer himself, a diary which was afterwards found to contain a practically complete account of the murder of Dr. Marshall and of the attempt upon the life of Gwendolen. But the document contained nothing, hardly a single detail, which was not anticipated by Jeffrey in the story he told me this morning.

"You remember," Jeffrey began, "the evening we dined together, and you found Jack Marshall waiting for you when we came back here? I left you immediately, for I don't know him well and felt sure he wouldn't want to speak to me. The desk clerk stopped me before I could get into the elevator and told me there was a gentleman waiting in the reception room to see me. It was Carlton Stancliffe, and I took him straight up to my quarters.

"I had never seen him before—not off the stage, that is—for the arrangement for the series of sketches and articles we were to do together had been completed through the magazine. It was a business call and I was expecting it. I no more imagined a connection between him and Dr. Marshall than between him and the Shah of Persia. But he had a newspaper with him and began to talk about the doctor. Told me how he had been there that morning; told me what was not in the paper, that it was supposed to be a case of murder. He also added that he was to go up to the office that evening to attempt to identify Pomeroy.

"Well, you may believe me or not, but it's true just the same, that before he got halfway through talking about the case, I knew he was the murderer just as well as I know it now. I can't tell you how I knew; I just saw the facts sticking out all over him, and I tell you it gave me a mighty queer feeling. After he had gone I did my best to throw it off. I told myself that it was a judgment on me for the mad things I had been saying to you at dinner. But for all that, the feeling kept growing stronger and stronger, and finally I went out and followed you up to the Marshall's house.

"I didn't reach there until after you and Jack had left, but Mrs. Marshall saw me. She is a remarkable woman. I hadn't intended saying a word to her, but before I knew it, she had my whole belief out of me. Of course she was incredulous. She knew nothing whatever about Mr. Stancliffe that would furnish any sort of conceivable motive for such a crime. Before we got through talking, however, the firmness of my conviction had had an effect upon her. On the other hand, her incredulity, together with her disclaimer of any personal acquaintance with Stancliffe, either on her part or the doctor's, had an effect upon me. I saw how utterly foolish anything I might say must sound, especially to you after the talk we had had that very evening.

"That perception didn't in the least affect my certainty that I was right, after all. So I decided on a course of action. I would say nothing more to anyone of this idea of mine—I pledged Mrs. Marshall to secrecy—but I would go to work, all by myself, to find out what motive Stancliffe could possibly have had for the murder, and how he could possibly have committed it.

"I got my first hint from you, yourself, when you came home late that night with the full account of your evening's adventures. You spoke then of the man Hyde whom Dr. Marshall had ruined, long ago, and my mind jumped at once at a possible identity between him and Mr. Stancliffe."

"Well," said I, "I wish you had been in my shoes from the first. We should have got to the end of our mystery a good deal quicker. I had a hint at that identity myself, but never perceived it, for when I was talking to Stancliffe about Hyde and how Madeline regarded him, he started, and knocked a siphon off the table. And two or three times when we were together he made the slip of talking like a doctor about hypnotism and other things. Then, too, the cool, scientific way he set about reviving Miss Carr when she fainted up in Dr. Marshall's office might have suggested a previous medical experience; only I appear to have been impervious to suggestion right along."

"It was all natural enough," said Jeffrey. "An actor is the most inconspicuous person in a community, just by reason of his semipublic character. You never think of asking questions about him. Of wondering what his real name is, or where he lived ten years ago, or what sort of moral character he has. He's the one sort of person in society who never has to account for himself. You think because you've seen him half a dozen times on the stage, that you know all about him.

"But, you see, I approached the case backward. I knew, *knew*—for I can't express that certainty strongly enough—that he was the actual murderer. With that knowledge I ought to have been able to build up a column of evidence that would support it. I fully expected that the evidence brought out at the inquest would prove to be valuable to me, and there I was sadly disappointed."

"It was made pretty clear," I observed, "that a doctor must have done it. That should have strengthened your conviction that Hyde and Stancliffe were the same man."

"Yes, that was well enough so far as it went, but it wasn't what I hoped for. I came away from that inquest in an execrable temper, because I was as much at a loss as ever as to how Stancliffe could have done it. I made the same mistake that everybody else did, namely, of assuming that because a whole series of patients—four, I think—were summoned in the regular way into the office, had their interview and went away satisfied, that Dr. Marshall himself must have been the person who talked to them, must have been alive and well after Stancliffe had gone out. I hoped to find a way in which he could have gone back from the corridor at some subsequent time before 12.30, and I wasn't able to find it.

"Just before you came in that evening I had received a note from Mrs. Marshall, which you chanced upon a little later, and which I fancy had the effect of directing your suspicions against both of us."

I had been waiting for him to come to that, and was feeling rather silly in anticipation of it.

"She wrote to me," Jeffrey went on, "solely out of regard for your feelings. She pointed out to me that it must necessarily be distressing to you to become aware that there was a confidential relation between herself and me in the case, from which you were excluded, and she suggested that, unless I wanted to take you completely into my confidence as I had herself, I should take care not to let you know that any such confidence existed. I meant, when you came in that night, to tell you the whole story, but you were off on another tack altogether, even hinting suspicion against Mrs. Marshall herself; so I closed up. I owe you an apology for that."

"I certainly owe you one," said I, "so if you don't mind, we'll let them cancel each other. But go on with your story; I want the rest of it."

"Well," said he, "I had no trouble in identifying Stancliffe as James Hyde, beyond all possible doubt. He posed for me the morning after the inquest, and I drew a sketch of him just as he was then. After he had gone, I went over it and made it about fifteen years younger. Just on the chance, I drew in the sort of mustache that everybody wore in those days, and took the thing up to Mrs. Marshall. It only needed one look at her face when she saw it, to settle all question of the identity.

"She told me then enough about him and about the trouble he had got into, to enable me to start an investigation of my own. She was only a girl of fifteen when it happened, and her version of the story couldn't be expected to be very complete.

"Hyde wasn't at all the wronged innocent that she thought him. He was a very brilliant man and a very fascinating man—that you will find it easy to believe—but he was almost utterly devoid of moral scruples. The thing that caused Dr. Marshall to drive him out of his profession and out of the city, was practically blackmail. He had used knowledge that came to him professionally to terrorize a woman. All the money she paid him, which was nearly all she had, was for alleged medical services, but it was blackmail just the same.

"The best thing about the man was, perhaps, his inability to see that there was anything wrong in what he had done. He simply hadn't any morals; that was all.

"I succeeded in tracing him as far as Australia, and then I managed to trace Carlton Stancliffe back from the same place. It was there that he drifted on the stage, and that was probably the profession that he should have followed from the first. There are very few men who enter that profession as late in life as he did who rise so quickly to eminence."

"Well," said I, a little bit resentfully, "when you knew all that, you certainly had something to tell me—any amount of fact and inference to justify your suspicion—and yet, without a word, you let me go blindly on, confiding in him, employing him, even, in the detection of the criminal."

Jeffrey laughed. "I *was* rather taken aback when I found that you had done that," he admitted, "but on second thought it occurred to me that it was the best thing that could have happened. The man would never be so completely off his guard; so completely unsuspicious that he himself was suspected as when he was serving you in that very employment. And keeping you in the dark as to what he really was simply made it possible for you to act naturally the part that you would have been compelled to play had you known the truth.

"During all those days while he kept you entertained with the evidence he was piling up against Miss Carr, I was racking my brains, and pretty nearly wrecked them, in an attempt to work out a sane and plausible theory of the murder. I never got it until you made that remark about the tobacco."

"That's what I've been waiting for all the evening," I cried. "How in the world did my remark about the smell of tobacco give you the clew?"

He stared at me, evidently incredulous that I could be so stupid. "Why," he said, "that's really in your department. It's simply a case of fact and inference. You said that Gwendolen Carr had remarked that the smell of tobacco in that office, more than the sight of the room itself, was what brought the terrible scene back to her. Well, of course, the odor wasn't that of tobacco, or was, rather, of a highly concentrated form of it. It was the smell of pure nicotine, the poison which the murderer used. Didn't you see Dr. Armstrong smell of that broken needle when the coroner handed it to him at the inquest? That's the only means he had of identifying the poison. Obviously, then, if Gwendolen Carr noticed that odor when she went in for her consultation with the doctor, it must follow that the murder had already been committed. And the man she talked to must have been somebody impersonating him. He could, of course, be no one else but the murderer."

"I see," said I, "but answer me another question. How did you know tonight that that syringe was to be found in Mr. Stancliffe's trousers pocket?"

"Think a minute," said Jeffrey. "What was the whole purpose of this second crime that Stancliffe was trying to commit out at Flatbush?

It was to prevent Gwendolen Carr from revealing the clew she unconsciously possessed that would have put us on his track: that, in the first place; and in the second place, to saddle an absolutely convincing proof of guilt upon her. How could he do it better than by secreting the instrument with which the murder was committed among her effects? But he couldn't do that safely until after she was dead. He probably carried it with him all the time, anyway. He could hardly have had a safer hiding place for it than upon his own person. There, now, I fancy you know as much as I do. You can reconstruct the rest of the story to suit yourself."

"No," I said regretfully, "I am afraid reconstruction is not my forte. Fill your pipe again and sit back in that chair, and tell me Stancliffe's story."

XVII

The Story is Told

"Why, in the first place," said he, "Carlton Stancliffe was a real actor, and he had a real trouble with his throat. Undoubtedly he went to Dr. Marshall as a perfectly *bona fide* patient, upon the recommendation of some other physician. Of course he knew who Dr. Marshall was, but perhaps the old enmity had died away; perhaps he was merely curious to see what the elder man would be like. He couldn't have been sure, of course, whether Dr. Marshall would recognize him or not, but, then, he wouldn't have cared much. His own success had been great enough to make him indifferent to the doctor's opinion of him; and as for any real shame or regret for the thing he had done, he simply never had any.

"Dr. Marshall must have failed completely to recognize him. I think that he must have told Hyde that his complaint was incurable, or at least have described it sufficiently, so that a man who was himself a physician of no mean attainment could have recognized the fact.

"Do you remember my telling you of Dr. Marshall's experience with a man who was doomed to go mad, and didn't know it? I am practically certain that Hyde, or Stancliffe, was that man.

"Now just imagine Hyde's feelings, sitting there in the office of his old enemy and learning that the disease he had thought lightly of was really incurable. Remember that it spelled absolute disaster to him in his new profession. He must have heard that verdict with despair.

"And not only despair, but something else. For the man who sat there behind the desk, sentencing him so coolly to what might about as well have been death, was the very man who had caused his former downfall. But for his—Marshall's—meddling in what was no affair of his, he—Hyde—might be sitting there at the other side of the desk, rich, famous, secure.

"Possibly Mrs. Marshall may have been an unconscious factor in the situation. It's altogether likely that he had seen her, had had her pointed out to him. He was a distant cousin of hers, remember, and very naturally, in that hour of despair, he counted her as rightfully his, as one of the things that the cool, confident, successful man across the desk had deprived him of.

"I think the idea of his ability to fill the doctor's chair and his place in society, his sort of potential right to possess all that the doctor possessed—I think it must have been with that idea that the notion of the crime came to him. Once it had come, it must have fascinated him. It was so perfect, so safe, and, to his mind, never well balanced morally, so perfect a piece of retributive justice, that to have it occur to him at all, was followed, as a matter of course, by his preparing to put it into execution."

"I am surprised that you should call it safe," I objected. "The idea of waiting there in the office for an hour or more, with the murdered body of his victim tucked away somewhere while he was admitting patients and talking to them in the character of the man whose life he had just taken, seems to me rash to the verge of madness. Either Dr. Armstrong or Miss Jerome could have come in at any time, and they would have detected him at a glance."

"But they wouldn't come in unless he summoned them. That's the point," said Jeffrey. "There's nobody whose privacy is so sacredly guarded as that of a physician in consultation with his patients. No, the only possible danger would come from some old patient of the doctor's who knew him well, and who would expect to be known. That danger, however, he obviated by waiting his chance. The beauty of the crime he was planning lay in this, that he need not make any move until a favorable chance presented itself. He had gone to the office twice before, that week, fully prepared to commit the crime he had set his heart upon, and only deferring it because he found that all the circumstances were not exactly to his liking."

"He told me once," I observed, reflectively, "that every well-planned crime had that particular merit."

"There is one thing I hadn't thought of, though," said Jeffrey, with a puzzled look. "How about his voice? How could he be sure that wouldn't go back on him? I should think that consideration might have upset the whole plan. Evidently it didn't; certainly not, at least, when he was talking to Miss Carr. But how could he be sure it wouldn't?"

"Well," said I, "he told me that his voice never failed when he was talking in another character than his own. He said that if he could only have made the managers believe it, he could have played his parts just as well as ever. That is the theory he diverted me with the night he smashed the siphon."

"Now, on that one morning," Jeffrey went on, "everything went beyond his hopes. He not only had a succession of patients behind him who he was able to ascertain were strangers to Dr. Marshall, he also had Pomeroy, and, unless I am mistaken, he recognized him."

"No doubt," said I; "he practically admitted as much to me."

Jeffrey looked at me with a rather rueful smile. "I do begin to regret your opportunities," he said. "At any rate, Stancliffe went into Dr. Marshall's office that morning fully fortified against mischance, and fully prepared for what he had to do. He knew exactly, as a result of previous visits, what the doctor's routine of examination was. He had studied out the exact moment when his chance would be best—when he was lying back submitting to examination, with Dr. Marshall bending over him. He had everything in his favor: a clever surgeon's skill and quickness, and a total absence of suspicion on the part of his victim.

"You know, from the testimony at the inquest, how that poison acts, and can imagine what happened, as well as I can. Dr. Marshall went down without a cry. The murderer then sealed up, with a piece of court plaster, the wound his needle had made. Then he proceeded, quite deliberately, to make up for the part he was about to play. Remember, he had all the time he wanted. He had no fear whatever of interruption.

"When everything was finally ready, he settled himself in the doctor's chair and rang for the next patient. He knew he was secure from detection. The next three patients who came in may not have received as valuable advice from him as they would have had from Dr. Marshall, but, at any rate, the impostor was a good enough physician himself to give them instructions and advice which they would never call in question.

"When he rang the bell the fourth time, he undoubtedly expected to see Pomeroy, and must have been a little taken aback when Gwendolen Carr came in instead. He had made the mistake of not seeing that the recognition between himself and Pomeroy had been mutual. But of course the moment Miss Carr told him who she was, namely, the young woman his son was anxious to marry, from that moment on, all was easy for him. All he had to do was to quarrel with her violently, to make sure that she should leave the office in a state of the utmost anger against himself, and the thing was done.

"Once he had dismissed her, the thing was all but accomplished. He had to remove his own make-up and conceal the traces of it; to drag the body of the doctor out of its hiding place and prop it up in the chair. That done, he could watch his chance to slip out into the corridor without attracting attention, and get away. I am sure that when he did so, he must have felt absolutely secure against detection.

"He was under no necessity to manufacture evidence, for he had what would protect him better—an irresistible presumption: the presumption that Dr. Marshall was alive when the bell rang that summoned Gwendolen Carr into his office.

"It was nothing more than a presumption for there wasn't a scrap of evidence to support it. The patients who followed Stancliffe were all admitted strangers. Armstrong testified that he had not been in since early in the morning. There was really some evidence against the presumption. Miss Carr told you that Jack had found it impossible to believe that his father would have said the things to her that she reported. Yet so strongly were our minds set in the other direction, that the only thing that occurred to us to do was to doubt the girl's veracity; never to dream for an instant that the person who said the things she reported might not have been Jack's father, but somebody else.

"Of course the girl's knowledge of her own innocence was a protection to Stancliffe, for he could rely upon her to tell the truth under questioning, in spite of the strength of the case she would create against herself by so doing.

"But right there occurred one little incident which he could not have foreseen: her testimony as to the hour at which she left the office. Her seeing the clock in the mirror and reading it backward left an interval of forty minutes vacant, and made possible the case against Armstrong. Of course it was to Stancliffe's interest that a sustained case should be made against somebody, and it was possible to make a better case against Miss Carr, when all the truth was known, than against Armstrong. Also, he could additionally safeguard himself by getting the credit of successful detective work.

"It must have been a queer game to play, pretending to make a series of brilliant discoveries of things he had known all along, but apparently he played it well. Neither of you suspected him, at least, that night in the office when he sprang his *coup* about the clock."

"Suspected him! I should think not," I exclaimed. "Gwendolen thanked him for having thought of it, and for clearing it up. For, of course, that was the one insoluble mystery between her and Jack."

"What did Stancliffe look like when she thanked him that night?" Jeffrey asked curiously.

"I remember now," said I, "I didn't see his face. He was staring out the window all the while, leaning back on his stick with his hands clasped behind him."

"Now, why in the world," said Jeffrey, "didn't she identify his hands then? She is the most observing young woman I ever saw."

"He wore gloves," said I.

"In spite of the fact that it was a hot night?"

"Yes," I admitted reluctantly. "There's another of the queer things I might have noticed."

"I understand," Jeffrey continued, "that you put it up to Stancliffe to decide whether she should be allowed to go home and remain quite free from surveillance, or not?"

"Yes," said I.

Jeffrey shrugged his shoulders and shivered a little. "I'm glad he's dead," said he. "He was a devil, if ever one walked the earth, and I shall sleep better tonight for knowing that he has gone to his reward."

"How did it all come to you, this account of the matter you've been giving me?" I asked. "Did it spring into your mind complete the moment I made that remark about the tobacco; or did it just grow up gradually, one detail at a time?"

"Why, I saw the main idea at once, of course, but I didn't know how to fill it up. The horrible danger that I knew Gwendolen Carr must be in at that very moment didn't leave much leisure for contemplating Stancliffe's past villainies. He was in process of carrying out a more diabolical scheme at that moment, and we had to be quick if we could hope to thwart him."

"I was hoping you would come to that," said I. "What made you think Gwendolen's life was in danger?"

"Why, she made that remark about the smell of tobacco to Stancliffe as well as to you, didn't she? Well, that told him she had in her hands the clew that would destroy him, although she herself didn't recognize it. But it was only a question of time before she would make that same remark to someone who would catch its import. So long as she was alive and in possession of that knowledge, his life couldn't be safe. Wasn't it after she made the remark about the tobacco that he told her she could go home alone?"

"Yes," said I.

"And she announced, didn't she, that she was going in the surface cars? Well, of course, that assured him of his opportunity to get out to Flatbush ahead of her. It was he, as I suppose you have guessed, who passed you on the sidewalk out there. Had you not been with her, he would, very likely, have killed her then and there on her own doorstep, and in some way to suggest that it was a case of suicide. Being foiled in that scheme, he simply thought of a better one; slower but surer."

"It seems to me," said I, "he ran a good deal of risk in taking a room there in her boarding house."

"I don't know," said Jeffrey. "His only risk was an encounter with her, which really must have been rather easy to avoid. And then, if she had seen him, she would have thought of nothing more than that he was playing the spy upon her."

"I still don't see exactly what he meant to do; what could he hope to do, unless he could literally scare her to death or out of her wits?"

"The only wonder to me," said Jeffrey gravely, "is that she wasn't found dead the second morning after you left her out there. Stancliffe knew, didn't he, that she had been taking something to make herself sleep?"

"Yes, she mentioned it to both of us."

"Well, what I suppose he did was this, and I should be greatly surprised if I proved wrong: he got into her room during her absence, and substituted for that packet of powders a number of perfectly neutral ones that could have no effect upon her whatever, and one at the bottom of the package which contained the concentrated dose that should have been distributed all through them. The natural thing for a person to do in her state of mind, half mad with terror and altogether in despair, would be to seek sleep at any cost. To take one powder after another, until she could get some effect. She would get no effect until she took the last one, and that would kill her. And when they found her in the morning, a half dozen empty papers would be taken for sufficient proof that she had committed suicide. When the suspicion which already pointed against her in the Marshall case came out, as it inevitably would, together with the discovery of the syringe, Stancliffe would have another irresistible presumption to fortify his first one with. It was the most utterly fiendish thing I ever heard of. And it was only thwarted by the incredible courage and sanity of that young girl."

We sat and smoked awhile in silence after that. Then I picked up the conversation where Jeffrey had dropped it. "Yes, she's the true metal. No doubt about it. What a veritable refiner's fire she has come through. She can't have known an untormented hour since she left her lover that morning, full of high hopes for the innocent ruse they meant to work on his father. Think what an accumulation of horror has been piled upon her since then. Shaken by Stancliffe's attack upon her, by her quarrel with Jack, tired out with the strain of the inquest. Then to have that white-faced, wild-eyed young lover of hers as good as accuse her of his father's murder. And to have that accusation backed up by facts that seemed to justify it! The only support she had was the consciousness of her innocence."

"Do you call that a support?" said Jeffrey. "I think it would have been easier for her if she had been guilty. If she had been guilty, she could have confessed and taken the consequences, and got the thing off her mind. It must have taken a good deal of courage not to confess, anyway; not to have made a lying admission that she had committed a crime that she was really perfectly innocent of. That happens sometimes, you know; happens, I believe, oftener than we suppose. But she isn't the sort of person to do a thing like that. She wouldn't make a lying confession, and she wouldn't destroy herself. She just sat tight and saw it through. I hope the man she marries will be good enough for her."

"He's in love with her, anyway," I said. "He's a good clean sort of chap. I think they'll be very happy."

Jeffrey assented rather grudgingly. "Well, he's got a heavy score against himself to make up. He's the one man who ought to have seen straight through the presumption that protected Stancliffe. When she told him things that he knew his father couldn't have said, he ought to have reached then and there the true conclusion, that the person who said them was someone else than his father. And when she said twenty minutes to twelve instead of twenty minutes past, he should have assumed that the clock was wrong."

"Well," I protested, "that's easy to say afterwards, but there certainly was evidence enough."

Jeffrey caught the word out of my mouth. "*Evidence?* There was evidence against every single innocent person in this case—Pomeroy, Armstrong, Gwendolen Carr. The only person against whom there wasn't any was the guilty man himself. No, evidence doesn't amount to much until it's tied on behind the right guess."

Then he laughed and stretched his arms. "Well," he said, "that takes us back to the point we started from, the very matter we were discussing before we read the paper with the account of Dr. Marshall's death in it. And as for me, I'm not going around the circle again. I've been around once, and that's enough for me. Stancliffe's dead, and I've fixed it up with the lieutenant to get Armstrong out. He's got all the facts necessary.

"I am going to sleep for three hours, and then I'm going to take a color box and go up to Bronx Park and paint, and the reporter or other person who thinks he's going to get another word out of me about the Marshall mystery is seriously mistaken."

"But," I protested, "you'll have to tell it once more, to Madeline and Miss Carr and Jack. You promised them a report at breakfast time, you remember; it's nearly that now."

"And do you think I've gone all over this once with you with the intention of serving it up again, *réchauffé*, over the breakfast table? No. From now on, anyone who wants to know anything about Dr. Marshall and the 'Whispering Man' will be gently but firmly referred to you."

I may take this occasion to observe that my friend has remained perfectly inflexible in this resolution. As a consequence, I have been kept telling the story over and over again, until now, in self-defense, I have sat down and written it out. Hereafter, anyone that wants to know about the story will be referred by me, in turn, to these pages, upon the last of which, or nearly, I hope I am now writing.

There is, indeed, but little more to say. At the earliest decent and reasonable hour I went up to the Marshall house, where I found Madeline superintending, as if they were babes in the wood, the breakfast of her convalescent stepson and his *fiancée*.

In answering the first of the eager questions they showered upon me, I am afraid I ruined my tale by beginning it wrong end to. But once their first curiosity was satisfied, they demanded the whole story from beginning to end, and I assenting, we adjourned to the library, the room where Madeline was first introduced into this tale, for the purpose.

The hour was still early and the spring morning not very warm, so the fire which glowed on the hearth had a good practical justification for itself. I should have held it justified had the room been stifling hot without it, just by the way it played over and caressed Madeline's face.

The two young lovers occupied the sofa at the farther side of the library, Jack, in consideration of the early stages of his convalescence, half reclining upon a heap of pillows, while Gwendolen sat near—oh, very near, and—Well, that needn't go into this story anyway.

The face I watched was Madeline's, as she watched them. I could hardly tell my story for looking at it. It was half eager, half regretful, yet wholly tender and all alight with a new understanding.

Jack took an even more severe view of his credulity regarding Gwendolen's guilt than Jeffrey had. Evidently it would take him a long while to forgive himself for not having seen the thing, which, now that it was past, seemed that it might have been obvious to all of us.

My recital was a heavy strain upon him, as, indeed, upon Gwendolen herself. So presently I cut it short, promising the rest at some later day.

I took my leave and left them in the library, but Madeline followed me down the stairs.

"Aren't they delicious?" she said to me, referring to the couple we had left behind. "Didn't it almost make the tears come just to watch them? I hope they'll be charitable and let me watch a good deal, for that's all I've got left. Well, it's something to get the real thing at last, even if it's at second hand. I've learned a good deal in two weeks, Cliff."

"Madeline—" said I.

But what I said to her, and what she said to me, then and afterwards, though not so very long afterwards—what she has been saying over and over again, ever since—what she said when, leaning over the back of my chair, she saw what I was writing on this page—is no concern, positively none, of any living creature in the world but our two selves.

The End

A Note About the Author

Henry Kitchell Webster (1875–1932) was an American novelist and short story writer. Born in Evanston, Illinois, Webster graduated from Hamilton College in 1897 before taking a job as a teacher at Union College in Schenectady, New York. Alongside coauthor Samuel Merwin, Webster found early success with such novels as *The Short Line War* (1899) and *Calumet "K"* (1901), the latter a favorite of Ayn Rand's. Webster's stories, often set in Chicago, were frequently released as serials before appearing as bestselling novels, a formula perfected by the author throughout his hugely successful career. By the end of his life, Webster was known across the United States as a leading writer of mystery, science fiction, and realist novels and stories.

A Note from the Publisher